The Children of the Crab

The Children of the Crab

by
André Lichtenberger

translated, annotated and introduced by
Brian Stableford

A Black Coat Press Book

ISBN 978-1-61227-200-9. First Printing. August 2013. Published by Black Coat Press, an imprint of Hollywood Comics.com, LLC, P.O. Box 17270, Encino, CA 91416. All rights reserved.

Introduction

Raramémé, histoire d'ailleurs by André Lichten-berger, here translated as *The Children of the Crab*, was first published by in Paris by J. Ferenczi in 1921. It was published shortly after Ferenczi had issued a new edition of Lichtenberger's *Les Centaures* (1904)[1], a novel with which it has strong thematic links. Indeed, the new preface that precedes *Les Centaures* in the 1921 edition is so much more appropriate to *Raramémé* that it is very diffi-cult to believe that it was not written to accompany the latter novel, and switched by Ferenczi when he decided to issue the reprint first.[2]

Raramémé might well have been written, or at least begun, some time before 1921, perhaps while the Great War was still going on. It could not possibly have been published during the war, in spite of its violent anti-Germanic sentiments, not merely because the censors would never have licensed its vitriolic comments about the fashions and attitudes of the French government, but because they would have judged, quite rightly, that its morose philosophical thrust was incompatible with the all-important project of maintaining morale.

---

[1] Available in a Black Coat Press edition as *The Cen-taurs*, ISBN 9781612271842.

[2] The preface to the 1921 edition of *Les Centaures* is included in the Black Coat Press translation; that volume also contains an introduction offering a brief account of Lichtenberger's life and career, whose details it would be superfluous to repeat here.

Whenever it was actually penned, however, the philosophical flight of fancy that the story develops and embodies was very obviously stimulated by the war, whose advent and progress must have prompted Lichtenberger to revisit and reconsider ideas that had previously fascinated him, not only when he wrote *Les Centaures* but when he wrote his doctoral thesis on 18th century socialist utopias. The latter study, some of whose materials were recycled in *Le Socialisme Utopique* (1898), inevitably takes a strong interest in the ideas of Jean-Jacques Rousseau and writers influenced by Rousseauesque ideas, but employs as its precursory starting-point a consideration of Aphra Behn's *Oroonoko; or, The Royal Slave* (1688), in which the indigenes of Surinam are imagined to be living in a Golden Age similar to the one that Rousseau subsequently credited to "natural" humans uncorrupted by civilization.

It is possible that the title *Raramémé* was selected as a kind of polysyllabic echo of Behn's; it is a trifle narrow as a characterization of the project, given that the principal point of the story is that the narrow collective of "Raramémé" is part of a several broader collectives, primarily and most crucially the one that binds the two children thus embodied, in a fashion that is simultaneously remote and intimate, to a complementary pair of "children of the crab." Whether or not it is the case that Lichtenberger's title is a faint echo of Aphra Behn, however, the story deliberately picks up the thesis whose crucial seed Lichtenberger's scholarly work detected in Aphra Behn and then tracked through the tradition launched in France by Rousseau, and it does so in order to bring that train of thought to a kind of elegiac culmination.

Les Centaures had already provided an elegy for an imaginary Golden Age, but had embedded its parable in the mythological matrix favored by many Symbolist prose writers, depicting a long-lost Arcadia of the Hellenistic variety, in which the ideal existence shared by the sovereign centaurs with fauns and tritons is callously crushed by humans who have mastered the elements of technology and civilization. *Raramémé* draws its inspiration, as many late-18th and early-19th century Arcadian novelists did, from anthropological fantasies erected on the basis of discoveries made in the Pacific by France's great navigators—especially the reports of the idyllic life of the Tahitians brought back by Louis-Antoine de Bougainville from his epoch-making voyage of 1766-69. It is thus enabled to integrate the death of its Golden Age into the current of contemporary history, sharpening the tragedy of its loss considerably.

While depicting a Polynesian island culture as a "missing link" between civilized human life and "natural" human life, Lichtenberger adds a further symbol in the form of a "missing link" of the biological variety, physically intermediate between humans and their nearest animal relatives, the anthropoid apes. It is not impossible that Félicien Champsaur, who published *Ouha, roi des singes* (1923)[3] two years after *Raramémé*, had read Lichtenberger's novel, and that it played some part in jogging his inspiration, but whereas Ouha is an obvious precursor of *King Kong*, Kouang, despite the similarity of his name and his giant stature, is definitely not. He is certainly a tragic figure, like Ouha and Kong, but his tragedy is very different in kind; unlike them, and in

---

[3] Available in a Black Coat Press edition. as *Ouha, King of the Apes*, ISBN 9781612271156.

common with the Oyas with whole society the plot brings him to co-exist, he is not infected by the slightest trace of *hubris*. He does not exhibit the slightest trace of Ouha and Kong's perverse extraspecific lust—and, indeed, provides a striking model of uxorious loyalty to his cruelly slain spouse.

Although *Raramémé* does not employ the same narrative strategy as *Le Centaures* in establishing a coherent and self-contained secondary world, not merely juxtaposing its hypothetical island with actual geography and history but entangling the two in a more complex fashion and most robinsonades, it is nevertheless a staunchly Symbolist work as well as a Rousseauesque philosophical fantasy. The additional complication also creates a certain confusion; whereas *Les Centaures* was a carefully measured and controlled work, however, relentlessly and majestically painstaking in working out the symbolism of its considered ecological mysticism, *Raramémé* is a patchwork, and the elements of the patchwork deal in extremes. It is a more reckless and far-reaching work than its predecessor, and might be thought by some readers to be reaching much further than anything it could possibly grasp—but that is an entirely virtuous endeavor, and helps to make the novel into a unique work of art: a masterpiece of sorts.

Although it is unique, the novel does have certain attitudinal and thematic affinities with earlier novels with which Lichtenberger might have been familiar, in addition to his acknowledged sources. Indeed, there is an entire subgenre of novels that employ remote tropical islands as crucibles for thought-experiments that attempt to weigh the extent and significance of the alienation of civilization from nature. Some of those in the English tradition, notably H. de Vere Stacpoole's *The Blue La-*

goon (1908), include motifs that are echoed in *Raramémé*. Lichtenberger's analysis is, however, a far more sophisticated and profound study than Stacpoole's, and very different in its central concerns, having no truck with the erotic issues central to *The Blue Lagoon* and such English predecessors as Ronald Ross's *The Child of Ocean* (1889) and C. J. Cutcliffe Hyne's *The New Eden* (1892) or the issues of environmental exploitation central to such novels as Douglas Frazar's *Perseverance Island* (1885). *Raramémé*'s story-line also has certain thematic connections with Edgar Rice Burroughs' *The Land That Time Forgot* (1918), which Lichtenberger is highly unlikely to have read, but the same comment applies; in terms of its philosophical ambitions and literary methodology, *Raramémé* is situated on an entirely different plane. The features that it has in common with the cited works are, however, of some interest as multiple reflections of ideas that were in adrift in the intellectual atmosphere of the period.

Raramémé is a book that probably could not have been written other than in the midst or the immediate aftermath of a Great War, prompted by the contemplation of a cataclysm. In spite of its Romantic Utopianism, it is a distinctly discomfiting narrative, and that is its purpose; any reader who cannot shed tears, in company with Kouang, while reading the climactic scene is manifestly less human than he is. The story is, in its fashion, a formal tragedy cast in the Classical mold, but it is also a very modern tragedy, which—until the evocation of its *deus ex machina*, and then only in a flagrantly sarcastic fashion—seeks no refuge in narrative distance, as Classical tragedies and commonplace modern transfigurations thereof usually do. It deals with hypothetical and fantastic materials, but it does not treat them as essentially *alien*, in the way that mythological fantasies—including fantasies that transplant their motifs into a contemporary context—usually tend to do. Lichtenberger's purpose is to treat its hypothetical constructions intimately and immediately, and he does so with a rare frankness and sensitivity. For that reason, the novel's philosophical fantasia is no less timely now than it was in 1921, even though the Great War that prompted it has been replaced in our everyday experience by different threats, in addition to the ecological holocaust whose continuation and intensification the story anticipates.

This translation was made from a copy of the Ferenczi edition. The copy in question is identified as one of the eighth thousand, which was a respectable sale for the time; of the five books advertised on the back cover for which editions are indicated in similar terms, only one—by the very popular Maurice Dekobra—is credited with larger sales to date. It is unclear why the copyright notice in that copy reads "Copyright by J. Ferenczi 192," as there is no obvious reason why the terminal digit should have been omitted or removed. The pages were uncut when I bought it, so it was presumably a left-over remainder copy rather than one that had been sold at the time of issue.

One feature of the translation that warrants preliminary comment is the treatment accorded to the songs. Normally, when translating French verse, I would render the literal meaning, discarding the untranslatable rhyme and scansion—albeit reluctantly—on the presumption that they are less important features. In the present case, however, the function of the rhyming and (slightly unsteady) scansion is one of implication—the fact that the doggerel verses rhyme in French can only be an artifice, as the originals are supposedly being sung in a Polynesian dialect. Logically, the French rendering must be sacrificing nuances of literal meaning in order to preserve the rhyme-scheme, so I have done the same. In some instances—most notably the crucial appeal to Kroum—French words are used for their onomatopoeic quality rather than their significance, and I have done likewise with the English words inserted in their stead. I have footnoted one improvisation where it was impossible to approximate a transfer of one meaning that does have an evident significance.

Brian Stableford

PROLOGUE

June 1914. A radiant afternoon.

Laurette de Vesnage is curled up in her wing-chair near the large bay window, wide open to the pink sky and the waveless ocean. Facing her, Captain de Pionne is turning his képi over and over between his fingers.

She is blonde, slim and delicately pretty, which melancholy creases in the corners of her mouth. He is tall, thin, brown-haired and well-built; he is a soldier. The family resemblance between them is, however, striking. There is the same bright blue gleam in the sharp and slightly close-set eyes, and there is the same curve, and a similar quiver, in the slightly flared nostrils. Half-turned toward the sea, one might think that they were sniffing the breeze in the same way.

"Then, this really is your last visit, Hugues?" she murmurs. "Your uniform makes me feel cold."

"Yes, Laurette," he replies. "I embark on Monday in Marseille, after getting my orders in Paris. I no longer have an hour to spare...I mean, to steal... from my duty."

She bows her head. "You've been very kind, Hugues, to give me this fortnight. I'm so happy that we were able to see one another again in this old house, where there are so many common memories of our childhood. It has been delightful to go for walks together once again, to recognize a few old faces together, to remember the game we used to play, and our arguments, and to take tea every afternoon under the gaze of the Uncle of the Crabs.

The Uncle of the Crabs... Hugues smiles. Both of them look at the walls, at a mediocre eighteenth-century portrait framed by exotic ancient arms. Luc de Vesnage, whose blood flows in their veins, and whose nose and blue eyes they have, was a thoroughgoing eccentric. A voyager, philosopher and naturalist, he sailed all the seas in pursuit of social and scientific truth, making bizarre observations and formulating ludicrous hypotheses as he went. Having departed with La Pérouse,[4] he disappeared with him. What remained of him was the memory of a crackpot, a few exotic objects more-or-less crumbled into dust, some marvelous sea-shells, illegible notebooks and a collection of water-colors, drawings and engravings representing all the varieties of crabs.

The pincers and carapaces of the crabs exercised a great prestige over the childhood of Hugues and Laurette. With a common accord, they agreed that, in honor of the Uncle of the Crabs, they would maintain

---

[4] Jean-François de Galaup, Comte de La Pérouse was a French naval officer appointed in 1785 by Louis XVI's Minister of Marine to lead an expedition to continue and supplement the Pacific explorations of Bougainville and James Cook, drawing up maps, opening up communications and collecting specimens for scientific research, before completing a circumnavigation of the world. The young Napoléon Bonaparte applied to go on the voyage but was not accepted—a decision that probably changed history, as is wryly and obliquely acknowledged by an unobtrusive detail in Lichtenberger's plot. La Pérouse sent back the documents relating to the early phases of his voyage when he repaired and resupplied his ships at Botany Bay in 1788, but they disappeared after setting off to carry out further explorations in March of that year. It was not until 1826 that wreckage of the ships was discovered on the coral atoll of Vanikoro; some of the artifacts were returned to France by Jules Dumont-d'Urville, who called at Vanikoro during the second of his three expeditions to the region.

amity with his people. Crabs were always exempted from the fishing expeditions in which, at low tide, bare-legged, they hunted in the rock-pools for crayfish, octopodes and fish. And it was doubtless also in memory of the uncle in question, who unites his pretty cousin with him, that the very young Sublieutenant de Pionne of the Colonial Infantry, one evening in Hanoi—many years ago already—permitted a local artist with slanted eyes to tattoo the blue crab on his wrist, which, pushing back his sleeve, he shows to the young woman.

"Laurette," he says, "You've admired the totem of our childhood on my arm. Before I go, let me give you its double." He hands her a dainty jade crab, scrupulous-ly carved by a stylet in Yokohama or Singapore. "Look at it sometimes in memory of me—in memory of us."

"I'll never be separated from it." There is an imper-ceptible tremor in her voice.

They both fall silent. They are both reliving the past. Orphans, second cousins once removed, they were brought together by the same old aunt in consequence of premature mourning, and brought up by her. She be-lieved that she was doing her duty when, Hugues having gone to Saint-Cyr, she devoted her final energies—the Vesnages and de Pionnes die young—to marrying off Laurette.

Oh, if only Hugues had declared himself when he left the École, when Laurette threw herself softly and delightedly into his arms! But timidity retained him, and pride—he was the richer of the two—and doubtless also an obsession with adventure inherited from Uncle Luc. He enlisted in the Colonial Infantry.

"When I come back, Laurette, I'll tell you some-thing..."

By the time he came back, Laurette, perhaps unconscious of her own heart, and perhaps vexed, had yielded to the insistences of Aunt Ermeline. For two months she had been the wife of that brute Paul Sajol, a sub-prefect with good connections, a future functionary of the comrades' republic. The two cousins scarcely saw one another, and only exchanged a few banal words.

Hugues left again. From time to time, by the hazard of a newspaper or a conversation with a comrade who had come from France, he caught echoes of the young woman's wretched life: her husband's excesses; the death of her daughter; and, finally, in the wake of a filthy scandal, the villain's disappearance, deported to an outpost in the Far East. Laurette then resumed her maiden name, without divorcing, and took refuge in her childhood home, in order to live there in solitude, or perhaps to die there. Her health had deteriorated considerably.

This time, Captain de Pionne had been unable to resist an impulse sprung from his utmost depths. He came to knock on her door. And for a fortnight, on twenty-four-hour passes from Saint-Jean-de-Luz, he has crossed the threshold every day.

Laurette murmurs: "Now that you're going away again, Hugues, I shall be completely alone again."

He shrugs his shoulders, and, with a hint of involuntary annoyance, he says: "Bah! You have friends."

She shakes her head. "You know full well, Hugues, that I'm alone."

It is true. He does know. Laurette Sajol has passed through so-called Society like a bright meteor that is subsequently swallowed up in the sea. Of her brief trajectory out of the shadows, Laurette de Vesnage has conserved nothing but dismay, and a need to disappear. "Society" has remained, for her, a nightmare of her marriage. She has always been a foreigner there. She was known there, jokingly, as "the feral child."

She has remained a "feral child." Apart from Hugues, she no longer has any family. A few banal and distant relatives hardly ever break the silence of her retreat with a visit or a letter. She is entirely pure, entirely alone with the evil that has put a blush on her cheeks and rings around her eyes.

Hugues repeats after her: "Yes, Laurette, it's true, you're quite alone… and it hurts me."

She sighs; two tears run slowly down her cheeks. "Oh, Hugues, Hugues! Before, after Saint-Cyr...why did you go away without saying anything to me?"

He makes an impotent gesture, chewing his moustache.

"We've spoiled our life."

If they were different people, perhaps they would attempt, in vain, to repair it, but their heredity of traditional provincial loyalty forbids them the deceptions by which others might seek forgetfulness or revenge. For them, adultery would not be simply adultery, but almost incest. They know that.

She raises her hand wearily and lets it fall back again. "You have your Tonkin, your jungle and your pirates, Hugues."

The officer makes an affirmative gesture with his chin. "Fortunately—and yellow fever too. But Laurette, I shall suffer more in thinking about you. And then again, you see, I'm going away from my country with an apprehension. After three months in France, I no longer have any doubt. I believe there's going to be a war."

She closes her eyes. At the edge of blue-tinged eyelids, the lashes flutter. "That would be terrible. It would be too terrible. It's isn't possible."

"Nothing is too terrible to be impossible," he replies; but he immediately goes on: "I beg your pardon. I swore to myself that I would only say cheerful things to you before leaving! Come on, Laurette, it's time for me to go pack my trunk; I entrust you, in our dear house, to the Uncle of the Crabs. Will you swear to me that you'll look after yourself?"

She holds out her hand to him. "Adieu, Hugues; I'll be very good. And you too, be very careful. Don't forget that you're carrying my entire family in your uniform."

He bows, and brushes her exceedingly slender fingers with his lips. She raises the jade crab to her own.

He leaves.

I. RARA AND MÉMÉ

An ardent red sun is sinking in the orange sky. In shadowy lairs, life wakes up and springs forth.

With brief lengthening bounds a band of kangaroos races down to the river. As it passes by, Tiparu the armadillo rolls up in his carapace and Kiwi, the flightless bird, emerges momentarily from his vague dream. Between the forked mango-trees, beneath the crows of the giant acacias, flying squirrels deploy their parachutes, launch forth and chase one another with shrill whistles. Immense flowers with variegated corollas embalm the atmosphere, some of them fluttering into the air: emerald, ruby and sapphire butterflies. Multicolored parrots chatter hectically.

Above the surface of the water peep the blue-green eyes and spoon-like beaks of water-moles. Pippi-kuink is in a fearful mood. As if he were conscious of his own strangeness he hides his frolics, his games and his amours.

Neither duck nor rat I deign to be,
I lay eggs have hair, a beak, four paws,
In the soft mud I plead my cause,
I amaze all and all amaze me.

Modest and awkward, the ornithorhynchi[5] emerge one by one from the reeds, their tails quivering, encour-

---

[5] The ornithorhynchus is nowadays better known as the duck-billed platypus.

19

aging one another, conscientiously dragging their little bellies over the sand.

Two bursts of laughter frighten them. They swerve, capsize, stumble, get up again, limping furiously toward the protective water. Terror! Two giants bar their way. Already reassured, however, they pause. They raise themselves up on their hind legs, agitating their fore-paws, sniffing and hissing, overwhelming Rara and Mémé with amicable but slightly undignified quacking sounds.

Slender statuettes, the two children are hand in hand. Light phormium loincloths scarcely cover their arched hips. Their bare limbs, the color of ripe apricot, have the flexibility of young wild beasts. Necklaces of red pandanus seeds and sea-shells hang down over their bronzed torsos, where blue designs, carefully tattooed, inscribe the nobility of their origin. Other complex blue webs ornament their foreheads and cheeks. Crowns of white flowers are posed on their shocks of black hair. A puerile gaiety sparkles in their symmetrical features, and from their delicately-shaped lips, between sharp white teeth, flows the most beautiful youthful and inextinguishable laughter.

With his harpoon, made with a sharp stone solidly encased in a straight stem, Rara scratches the sand in front of the most adventurous of the amphibians, which understands the game and tries madly to grab it. Already, however, the rest of the band is jostling around Mémé, who is sitting down. In a broad latanier leaf she has brought a provision of snails, slugs and mud-worms, and is distributing them. From time to time she pauses, teases them, pretending to bargain; they nibble her angri-ly, sitting up on their backsides, protesting with hectic hissing sounds. Then, once again, their beak-like mouths extended, clapping desirously, they consume the food greedily.

In water and on land, Pippi-kuink run, run.
In water and on land, Pippi-kuink guzzle, guzzle.

In the battle for the provender, the less nimble lose their equilibrium, falling on their backs. There are frenetic wrigglings, which extract further laughter from the children. The stout Pippi, the father of the tribe, squanders thrusts of his hips in vain trying to regain his stance. Rara tickles his belly with the tip of his harpoon. The offended Pippi bites the stem, choking with rage. Around him, his offspring complain noisily to the gods.

Finally, Mémé's bare foot comes to the patriarch's aid. He completes his reestablishment and draws away, very dignified, wagging his tail. All his fellows follow him. Mémé's hands are empty, in any case. The unexpected fall of a calabash hastens the stampede. In the crown of a coconut-palm, white-maned monkeys are carefully stripping the nuts and peppering the runaways with the peel.

Hand-in-hand once again, Rara and Mémé, a song on their lips, walk along the stream. Its flow is clear and noisy, between banks covered in medeoloides lilies. Under their feet, water-snakes and tiny turtles swarm. Fantastic tree-ferns, clumps of mulberries and guavas frame them with their prodigious verdure. Sleek blue dragon-flies glide over the water, brushing them and taking flight.

Gradually, the foliage thins out and becomes stunted. The waves hasten, breaking and foaming. There is a barrier of rocks through which, in the distant past, the waters laboriously scoured a passage. The broken flanks

21

of the cliff are ablaze with red orpiment and the ardent greens of malachite. The children are up to their knees in water.

Between their calves, among the large gray shrimp, are the golden and steely flashes of fish.

The gorge narrows. The torrent rumbles more deafeningly. There is a chilly odor. In the shadows, glittering stones alternate with holes full of darkness. Here and there, in the fissures, bats are mewling. A cavern yawns, in which colossal bones are whitening. Piously, Rara raises his fingers to his lips, and salutes with his open palm the remains of the giant birds that were kings before the humans, and whose spirits it is appropriate to appease. Mémé reproduces exactly the same gestures.

The gorge is already broadening out again. A sheet of orange sky is revealed, and also, high up, the bleakness of the basalt, on which a mast is erected. A striped flag is fluttering there.

While continuing to paddle, Rara and Mémé honor the divine sign, and sing their tribute:

The livid gods are feared by the light of day,
The water spat them out and took them away.
They will come back from the distant blue;
Where their feet once trod, the earth is taboo.

Above the chant of their childish lips, however, rises the murmurous growl of the sea. The last expanses of the wall crumble. Liberated, the stream spreads out nonchalantly over the golden sand, where it is united with the caressing waves.

The virgin wind, which nothing except for vast albatrosses and gigantic frigate birds has breathed in for thousands of kilometers, blows over bronzed faces. A wide open bay is limited by two rocky points. To the left, in the background, a peak is outlined, surmounted by a thick column of smoke. Rara's index-finger points to it.

"The spirit of Hakarou is agitated."

"May Hakarou be blessed," Mémé replies.

The black heads of coral protrude here and there from the steep shoreline. Beyond the most distant, a brown islet, unexpectedly emerged, launches two water-spouts toward the sky and sinks, leaving behind a wake of foam.

The children shout, in chorus:

Good hunting to you, Harka the whale
Good hunting to you, thank you for your gift.
To us of your scraps, Harka the whale,
Good hunting to you, spit out your spindrift.

When Harka idles close to the shore, the fish take fright and are abundant on the reef—but the tide is still too high. The children sit down on the golden sand, amid the wrack, the coral debris and the shells. Mémé curls up against Rara's side, leans her head on his shoulder and says, coaxingly: "Tell the story of things again."

And Rara, having stuck his harpoon in the sand, condescendingly intones the Polynesian genesis.

The tradition is deposited in Mémé's mind exactly as it is in his, but in order that the revered images that come from the ancestors shall not be effaced, it is good that the words, hymned according to the rituals, should project them into the light. From the boy's lips spring formulas inculcated by the sages. Mémé accompanies them with gestures, finishes the sentences or repeats the conclusions as a chorus. It is a cantilena for two voices that are only one, since Rara and Mémé are only two halves of Raramémé.

Once, there was Atua, the Eternal Night.[6] But Rahuo became bored, and, from the soft and diffuse Entity, by means of the great fish-hook, pulled out Oaleya, the fortunate island. He seated it solidly in the waters, set plants upon it, filled it with animals and pinned the sun and moon in the sky to illuminate it. In the beginning, their movements were hasty and disordered, but the subtle Mawi fixed them with the jawbone of his grandfather, in such a way that thereafter, the sun, as it went down, caused the moon to rise, and their march became slow and regular.

Higher up is placed the reservoir of the rains, and higher still the winds. Even higher are the redoubtable spirits, after that the light, and then the ultimate sky, in which Rahuo, king of the gods, is resident.

Rara pauses. Golden sand runs through his brown fingers. Mémé articulates the response: "But the gods are everywhere."

Rara nods his chin, throws back is head and resumes.

The gods are everywhere. They fill the earth, and that which is underneath, and the waters, and the skies. Some are visible, others invisible. Some are good and others evil. The wise know words that attract them, repel them, conciliate them, constrain them, or even kill them.

---

[6] In the language of Samoa, Atua means "god," and the term is often used as a plural to refer to the gods of Polynesian peoples in general, so Lichtenberger's appropriation of the term is highly idiosyncratic. Rahuo is an improvisation, as is the rest of the mythology of the Oyas, although it contains obvious echoes of actual Polynesian mythologies.

Killing them all would be the safest thing, but that cannot be done; so it is necessary to charm them with incantations and appease them with sacrifices.

Among all the islands with which Rahuo's whim has strewn the great water, Oaleya is the most privileged, but there are three others almost as spacious, or four, or perhaps ten; bold minds think that there might even be more, but that is improbable. Oaleya shines by comparison with them like the sun by comparison with the palest of the stars. So, in great pirogues, the chiefs brought all the superb Oyas there: men and women, the people of the crab, the people of the armadillo, the people of the kangaroo and the people of the octopus...

Outside of Oaleya the Fortunate, where the Oyas are, only miserable tribes exist, half-human, half-animal, without blazons, clinging to their reefs as best they can, like limpets.

From the soft Entity that surrounds everything that is, anything might surge. All kinds of apparitions emerge therefrom, to be reabsorbed again. There are famous ones that sometimes possess human form, the pallor of the surf, the mastery of the lightning and the most disconcerting magic. Their coming presages great cataclysms, which it is appropriate to welcome with resignation, for they are unavoidable, and they pass. Everything about them is taboo, including their slightest signs and traces. Toward the mast that dominates the bluff—where the blue, red and dirty white flutter—four thin bronze arms are raised, and childish voice shout:

Fear the livid gods who bring dismay
The water spat them out and took them away.
They will come back from the distant blue;
Where their feet have trod, the earth is taboo.

Mémé repeats, with a fearful expression: "They will come back."

"They will come back," Rara confirms. "But what does it matter?" he adds, proudly. "We are children of the crab."

Along the edge of the swaying coconut-palms, a young man and a young woman are walking, their foreheads crowned with tiaras, and there little fingers linked. Yesterday, they were living amid the tribe. Now they are going to construct their hut of woven leaves. They extend their open hands toward the children: "Blessed is the crab."

Raramémé reply, in chorus: "Blessed the armadillo."

According to the blood from which they have emerged, and the dispositions testified by their minds, young Oyas, in their fourth spring, are marked with the sea-urchin, the armadillo, the crab, the bird of paradise, the kiwi or one of the other animals of the elect. Thus is fixed their parentage and their character. Tupo and Maila are children of the armadillo, which places them in an honorable rank, but Raramémé are children of the crab, as the glorious blue totem inscribed on their breasts attests; thus their blood is the most divine, for Rahuo is also the Great Crab—and instead of being separated in two intelligences, their soul is one.

With a slightly disdainful compassion, their eyes follow the young couple who are drawing away. By Rara's side, Mémé whispers, with pride and self-satisfaction: "Only those born united are truly united."

Indeed, it is in vain that others seek one another, coming together and contracting temporary bonds in the fashion of beasts. Two intelligences subsist in them.

They are two lives, consecrated to two destinies. To the children of the crab it is given to be one in two bodies.

Before being marked, Raramémé had but one cradle in a single huge shell, and were nourished by the same teats. The sign that was conferred upon them by Manga-Yaponi, the old sage, only consecrated the manifest election of Rahuo. They have two heads, but one brain. If Rara coughs, Mémé feels a pain in her chest. When she goes away, he suffers an amputation. They wake up simultaneously, are hungry, thirsty and go to sleep simultaneously. They will extend their lips to the Black Flower simultaneously. By virtue of a special politeness, Rara has given Mémé his right arm, which is so strong; Mémé has given Rara the gentle little warm beast that beats beneath her left breast; but that is just a game. All of Rara is Mémé; all of Mémé is Rara. There is Raramémé.

In the times when the gods were less jealous of Oyas, the crab clan was very numerous. Today, there are only the two children, so they are tenderly venerated by their people. It is only the people of the octopus that continue to separate from them the old hatred that once made enemies of Kroum, the armored king with the strong claws and the sly Glonsk, the pulpy carcass with the viscous arms. The people of Kroum and the people of Glonsk never sit down to eat together.

It is because of the atavistic malediction in question that the squinting Mao, when he perceives the children as he crosses the strand, makes a detour to avoid contact with them. They have spotted him, however, and mock him: "Good hunting, octopus—look out for jellyfish!"

Of all the prey of the sea, the jellyfish, its carcass crystalline and opaline in the sunlight, is the most disdained.

Mao turns his head away, spits sideways, and points two fingers at the jeering pair to curse then. They laugh more uproariously and ward off his curses by turning their golden palms toward the sun.

But the sun is slowly sinking toward the horizon. The gulfs have sucked in the salty waters. The jagged coral is outlined in all directions. In their lattices and festoons the swarming life of the sea remains captive.

Sometimes wading waist-deep in the water, sometimes leaping from rock o rock, sometimes swimming a few lengths, Raramémé have reached the great reef, and proceed with the collection of sometimes-baroque mollusks, crustaceans and juicy algae.

In the thickets of the fortunate isle there are fruits, roots and other living things to maintain their life, but the children of the crab are fonder of the iodized and salty seeds of the sea than the impoverished and insipid seeds born of that morsel of dried-out sea, the land.

With a cry of triumph, Rara hauls out a jack mackerel that he has just harpooned. Mémé runs up to grab the tail and tear it with beautiful teeth. To tease her, Rara holds it over her head. She lets go, falls backwards, disappears into the water, reappears some distance away, shakes her soaked tresses, laughs, shouts, and dives repeatedly in pursuit of frightened turtles. Fifty meters away, however, a fin cleaves the surface of the torpid waves.

Mémé utters the warning cry: "Harrah!"

Flapping his arms and legs, Rara sends foam flying and regains the shore, swimming precipitately. He hoists himself out briskly, and, streaming, mocks the shark, tempted and disappointed. Mémé complains tenderly: "My arm hurts." As he landed, Rara has scratched himself on the spurs of the coral. She puts her lips on the wound in order to extract the evil spirit, only pausing to insult the shark—which continues prowling—with all the wrath of her puerile mouth, from which Rara's blood trickles in a thin thread.

Raramémé search the great reef, the scrupulous millenarian work of madrepores, with their subtle noses, their sharp eyes and their agile hands. Between the emergent calcareous slabs, magical submarine palaces conceal a prodigious pullulation of creatures, forms and seeds. In mysterious forests with perspectives of indefinite shadows and bizarrely-contorted trees, pink, mauve and blood-colored branches proliferate, where indescribable foliages hang down and float, in which paradoxical fish and improbable crustaceans nest. Among the tresses, plumes, manes, spokes and clouds, stars scintillate, some of which are flowers and others beasts. Countless mollusks—jewels with infinitely various spirals, delicate, baroque or obscene marvels—yawn or crawl, radiant with all the colors of the rainbow.

Pincers and antennas extend from the orifices of lairs, where carapaces twitch. Predators lie flat, in ambush, and leap forth. Some of them are all head and mouth; others all stomach. Some are bristling with spikes, like chestnuts, others so flat that they are invisible in profile. Some are as dazzling as sapphires or emeralds, others confounded with the sand, stones and mosses. They project spears, saws, tentacles, fins, tails, horns, or the most deformed and inexplicable excrescences. Here and there, flying-fish with scarlet wings take flight fearfully, and fall back with a splash, fluttering desperately.

It is the fecund and inexhaustible flourishing of the sea, in which today's harvest is renewed and tomorrow's is growing. Only a few hundred kilometers from the fortunate isle, bottomless abysses are hollowed out in the ocean, closed to human curiosity. The animals and plants that our eyes have seen are excluded therefrom. A sealed, secret, inaccessible matrix, where what will be is perhaps slowly marinating below what is. In the air, the volcano Hakarou is scattering his heavy swirls. Of the millenarian collaboration of the madrepores and the central fire, that fugitive parcel, Oaleya the fortunate, was born. Perhaps, scarcely ten thousand years ago, it was still asleep in the gulfs. Perhaps, in another ten thousand years, it might sink again, or—who can tell?—might cleave the sky with a snowy peak.

The children sprawl on a bed of wrack. Their hunger appeased, they are no longer swallowing any but a few choice delicacies. By means of a long fish-bone, Mémé extracts a violet slug from its speckled shell and offers it to Rara. Rara offers her a couple of fat oysters, whose greenish flesh surrounds an opal cushion. But his dark eyes light up...

Mémé's foot is dangling in an irregular pool whose bottom is invisible. Toward the transparent surface, the tip of a thong extends from far below. It is twisting, undulating, making sly progress; now another becomes discernible, similarly sliding. Rara whispers something in Mémé's ear. She remains lying down, nonchalantly, looking out of the corners of her eyes, negligently playing with hr amber ear-lobes. His lips taut, harpoon in hand, Rara climbs up on the rock, reaches an overhanging point and leans over. Three or four hideous serpents are extending avidly toward the tempting flesh: it is him!

A filthy bag inflates at the mouth of a cavern. Horrible eyes embellish the head-cum-belly. All of it moves with an atrocious flexibility and nightmarish velocity Rara throws his right arm back, balances his harpoon, hurls it with all the forces of his muscles, and, with a cry of triumph, hauls on the phormium cord. A monstrous star-flower emerges, bristling with pustules and helmeted with a tangle of vipers. The tentacles hiss, slap, twist and cling, struggling. One of them coils around Rara's arm, sticks there, and its thousand suckers pump his blood with powerful suction. Two others attempt to bind is legs. But Mémé has leapt upon the beast; her two nimble fists have already gripped the viscous pocket, twisting it victoriously. Sagging and blind, the mass of jasper flesh is in its death-throes, with frightful palpitations, on the coral platform. The two children take one another by the hand, and execute a mocking dance around it.

> Glonsk slides and winds,
> Glonsk sucks and binds.
> Suck this, suck that, Glonsk is there,
> > On the ocean bed
> > His belly-head
> > Extends and takes
> > With his eight snakes
> > That swarm and seek
> > And coil and streak;
> > Beware, your lusts,
> > My harpoon thrusts,
> Whistles, hisses, lashes, cracks
> Mine the stone and mine the ax.
> Die, Glonsk of the snaky gyve!
> Have no fear! Kroum is alive!

With all the might of their young lungs, the brown children repeat the centuries-old call over and over again: "Kroum is alive! Kroum is alive!"

And now, just as their young forms were once outlined on the surface of the waves, when Rahuo, the Great Crab, took existence from the eternal night and inscribed his image thereupon, so, to the call of their race, the blue crabs wake up, moving in their holes, clicking their pincers and running at the oblique trot of their eight legs. In a matter of seconds, the entire rocky promontory has come to life. There is a host of steely carapaces rolling, gliding, bumping into one another, climbing over one another. Some are smaller than snails, others larger than giant tortoises. Some are smooth and polished, mirroring the final rays of the setting sun; others are rough and rugged. Some are covered with fleeces of moss from which beards and wigs hang. All of them assemble around the children, beside the dead octopus, jostling in a rattling circle.

Waving their arms rhythmically, they intone a hymn:

Click, clock
Crock, knock
In the deep
Are we asleep?
Something's died
Let's climb outside;
Blood will revive,
Kroum is alive![7]

---

[7] The final couplet is this version of the song, repeated three times, is *Sang fait du sang,/Kroum est vivant* [Blood makes blood; Kroum is alive]. The former line is not invariable in later renderings, however, when lines encouraging the use of such rhymes as "revive," "arrive" and "survive" are used; given their general propriety in the context of the plot it

Click, clock
Knock, block
In my claws
Everything scores
Rips and cries
Cuts and dies;
Blood will arrive,
Kroum is alive!

Click, clock,
Block, mock
Shall we go
Back down below?
To take our pride
Away to hide;
Blood will survive!
Kroum is alive!

In each verse, at the moment when Raramémé utter the chorus, the entire horde raises its pincers, clicking the two halves together, bulging eyes gleaming.

The children fall silent and make the authorizing gesture: "Go!" Within a matter of seconds, the jostling wave has broken over the carcass. Mandibles grasp the hard flesh, ripping it apart, scattering it and swallowing it.

But the spirit of the sea, resting in the deep abysses that it has hollowed out, has become fat and swollen again. Here it comes, with an enormous soft murmur,

---

seemed reasonable to use them here as well, in the absence of any rhymed improvisation closer in significance to "blood makes blood."

from far away, rising up and licking the coral, soaking it with saliva and covering it up.

The children have returned to the beach of golden sand, and collapse there lazily. A great peace hangs in the limpid evening air.

A roseate breath bubbles beneath the smoke of Hakarou. The sea purrs. On the edge of the coconut palms, the last trills of the songbirds die away. Breezes pass by. The nocturnal phantoms are doubtless preparing to make their rounds. With their open palms, the children ward off the jealousy of the dead.

Busily, they proceed with their toilette, scrubbing one another, grooming one another and pampering one another. They have washed their bodies carefully and rubbed them with fine sand and handful of odorous herbs. With the aid of long thorns they part and smooth their hair. With agile fingers, Rara arranges Mémé's hair into symmetrical bangs. He polishes her cheeks and shoulders with a clump of juicy fucus. She carefully cleans his teeth, ears and fingernails, whose asperities she pares away with incisive thrusts.

They are so absorbed in their task that they pay no attention to the strange form that has just surged from the forest and is descending in their direction with an uneven gait. In Oaleya the happy, an individual does not rise up in hatred against his fellows. The gulfs between species, insurmountable elsewhere, are not hollowed out. Kour, the coral, is both stone and beast. Raina, the sea-anemone, is both flower and cephalopod. The plant Pakoa devours insects. Kiwi, the hairy bird, has no wings. Hapi, the squirrel, is akin to a bird. Pippi-kuink, the duck-billed mole, suckles young that hatch from eggs. Tiparu the armadillo is both tortoise and rat.

In Oaleya the fortunate, what is the hairy giant who is advancing on two feet, supporting his limping tread with a crutch?

He is undoubtedly an ape, more formidable that the most formidable in Africa or Malaysia. The colossal width of his torso, the length of his arms and its gait—his entire appearance—is reminiscent of the gorillas and the orangutans. He is a bear in the power of his neck and spine, the thickness of his limbs and its fleece, the growl rumbling in his torso.

Is he not entirely human, though? There is no muzzle, but a flat nose. Beneath the surmounting thatch, the commencement of a brow must lodge an embryo of thought. His legs are not terminated by hands or paws, but by human feet, save for the claws that terminate the toes.

And now that they have perceived the children, the eyes, previously unexpressive, light up.

Herr Klagenmeyer, if you saw the fame radiating there, how would you classify your former captive?

At the sound of his heavy, limping step, the children turn their heads, clap their hands and bound toward the newcomer like young domesticated dogs, leaping up to greet him.

"Kouang! It's the Hairy One."

They surround the hirsute mass with their capers, tugging at his arms, hanging on to his legs, climbing on to his back. The monster lets himself fall to the ground, groaning. Now they are rolling around with him, heads over heels. They get up again with volleys of laughter, grabbing handfuls of coarse hair, pinching him, manhandling him, climbing over him. A single excessively heavy blow from the gigantic limbs could crush the children, a flick could tear them into shreds, but the individual allows the teasing to proceed, with a faint purr. Astride the nape of his neck, Rara twists a crown of seaweed around his temples. Mémé offers him a calabash of fresh water, into which she has squeezed the juice of an orange. He drinks it without lapping, holding the vessel in his fingers, the palms of which are pink, like those of negroes.

The suave shadows fall. There is no longer anything in the sleeping woods but the sparse ululation of night-birds. With shrill whistles, silky bats are chasing one another. The glimmer of the volcano becomes redder beneath the pitch-black dome. But what murmurous apocalyptic drone, drawing nearer, is filling the atmosphere with a thunderous hum? Kouang, shrugging off the children, who fall backwards, comes to his feet with a single bound, Mouth open, breathless, his hair bristling, he challenges the unknown raptor, whose wing-span surpasses that of a condor...

Indifferently, the seaplane flies over the shore, changes course, and goes back out to sea. In a few seconds, it is no more than a black dot in the red stripe of the twilight.

Rara and Mémé have risen to their feet and, palms open, are saluting the spirit that is floating over the waters, among so many others—for it is the hour when souls, breaths and germs agitate tumultuously in the fortunate isle. Alongside the visible life, an entire invisible life quivers. Only the insane dare plunge themselves into adventure there. The wise are wary, and at least take care to swathe themselves in efficacious talismans that do not permit them to be confronted.

In the distance, over the southern headland, the spirits of the dead are palpitating. For three days they have remained languid, prowling around perishable bodies;

then, obedient to Rahuo's order, they have been definitively torn away and are shivering as they await the typhoon that will carry them away. In the meantime, when night falls, they wander around the island, rustling in the foliage, drinking from springs, drifting over the marshes, leaning over sleepers.

Friend, do not becoming imprudently drowsy near stagnant water; escaping from your lips; your breath risks being captured by the spirits of the dead. You will wake up demented, or will not wake up at all.

If you have eaten the liver of a shark, if a heart of brass lodges in your breast, if old sage Manga-Yaponi has furnished you with the most powerful charms, that is the only moment when you might take the risk. Light a fire, throw flowers and cut grass on it according to the rites, pronounce the formulas that the ages whisper in the ear tremulously; the tamed gods will be constrained to come, and perhaps, from inconceivable gulfs, that which remains of the dead. That is the moment at which you might be able to communicate with those who were, and who perhaps still are, at least to a tiny degree.

That is the moment at which you might be able to communicate with those who will be—and who already are, for nothing upon the earth is born or disappears; everything exists eternally. The eternal homogeneity circles around you, indefinitely. The humans of today are only the passing faces of the humanity that, like the legendary serpent, is indefinitely swallowing its own tail.

On the northern edge of the pool of Taroa, the souls of the children that you will bring into the world are quivering invisibly, as well as those of their children and their great-grandchildren. Like impalpable moths, furtive dragonflies, iridescent bubbles, smokes, breaths, dusts and pollens, they float at the whim of breezes, swirl and steal away.

Husband, with your head crowned with gardenias, if you have built your hut, if you desire a newborn to open its eyes to you in Oaleya and perpetuate your totem, go hand-in-hand with your wife, kneel down beside Taroa and accomplish the vigil of souls. If it pleases Rahuo, your watch will not be sterile.

At this hour, the men and women gather around old Manga-Yaponi, crouching outside his hut, and they collect the precepts of his wisdom, the magic words and the talismans that his great age and experience have accumulated within him. For at this hour, attracted by the fire of dry bracken that he has lit, and which he maintains incessantly, mingling fetishes and aromatic herbs therein, all the spirits have come to flutter amid the flames.

The air that surrounds him is charged with the spiritual and the divine, as the spring breeze is charge with the perfume of roses. Skillfully, no matter how far they have come or how subtle they are, the old man captures the spirits, inhales them, distills them, digests them; and from his lips run torrents of precious honey. He proffers science, history, wisdom, healing and curses. Any question formulated falls into him as into an inexhaustible well of knowledge. He draws inestimable advice from it, perpetually. He grips the ungraspable, feels the impalpable.

Through his voice, the gods and the ancestors speak. Of the invisible he makes the visible; that which is no more is renewed, thanks to him. Perhaps other islands exist in the sea. There might be as many as ten of them, and perhaps more, but they are miry, miserable and diffuse regions; their substance is scarcely more tangible than that of the clouds that assemble in the sky and disperse there. If humans live there, they drag out a poor and incomplete existence.

Oaleya is the navel of the world, the center of existence. To tell the truth, it alone exists fully. People are only entirely alive while their feet are upon it; they begin to die as soon as they move away from it. At the moment when they pass over the horizon, they dissolve once again into the soft and uncertain Entity in which everything was before Rahuo became bored and created the world in which everything remains that his gesture has not withered.

Thus, the destiny of Oaleya and the Oyas that live there has earned them the jealousy of all the gods. It is not impossible to take them by surprise, to dupe them or disarm them with artful incantations, but Oaleya, which was born of the caprice of Rahuo, will return to mud at the caprice of his whim. In the bosom of universal being, it is only a very tiny thing. Around it, death prowls with a thousand face; within it, it nourishes death.

Once, the people of Oyas were innumerable. They are still innumerable today, for what brain is sufficiently robust to count them? But when Manga-Yaponi's hair was black, the men and women of the tribe, squatting in the evening, covered all the terrain that extends from the chief's hut to the great hibiscus thickets. Today, half that area is sufficient to contain them all. Some poison is undoubtedly undermining the strength of the Oyas, exhausting and rarefying them.

That is a little sad, but it is not appropriate to be excessively afflicted by it. Before humans, very probably, the Moas, the great birds, were kings of the island. They have disappeared. The Oyas will likewise disappear. Perhaps, in their place, the pale gods will reign, or even the kangaroos. Or Rahuo might dissolve things completely; everything might return to the sea, and only Kroum will survive. That does not matter much. It is appropriate that everyone, unless they are mad, should await their destiny cheerfully.

In the meantime, of course, it is permissible for us to anticipate it. It might even be excellent. For, although the point is somewhat lacking in precision, it is quite plausible that somewhere, Rahuo has forged another blessed isle. Not much is known about it, except that out there, perhaps, other bodies might exist whose stomachs are larger and limbs more robust than those of the Oyas. There is reason to think that instead of floating, the play-things of typhoons, the souls of great chiefs and those who have been able to equip themselves with the most efficacious charms will succeed in joining them, in being reincarnated there, thus to taste once again, more ardent-ly, the pleasures of love, of feasting and all the rest...

It therefore happens sometimes that not only those who are tormented by evil demons, but those animated by hardy—albeit somewhat presumptuous—souls seek the Black Flower prematurely; they have more chance of succeeding in their hazardous migration, being more ro-bust, more able to struggle hard against the jealous pow-ers, and perhaps able to capture younger and healthier forms, in order to lodge therein.

Minniloa, with the petals the color of night, flour-ishes under the great thickets of lataniers near the south-ern banks of Taroa. It is there that the sick and the old go painfully in quest of it, and sometimes, buoyantly, the amorous and reckless young hunters who brave the ad-venture. It is preferable that you gather it on the night that follows the full moon. You take it in the morning to Manga-Yaponi, the wise old man. All day, he pounds and kneads it in a calabash with other herbs, turtle-blood and the juice of certain mollusks, while pronouncing the formulas of which he has the secret. In the evening, he warms the mixture on the fire before which the tribe is assembled. At his command, the deadly principles complete their incorporation within it.

Take up the cup; empty it. Now you will sink into the great sleep and, the next day, your body will lie inert forever, unless the red ants have already covered it with their bandage. What will become of your soul? That is the mystery. If you miss your chance, weary of waiting in vain on the southern promontory, it will wander indefinitely through the woods, at random, and its plaints will frighten the living forever...

The night, the immense tropical night, has expanded. In the black sky, dense clusters of stars are ablaze in the infinite. The sea is similarly flamboyant. In myriads and myriads, the zoophytes have lit their fires. The entire surface of the calm waters is phosphorescent. Harmonious life is sweating, respiring, humming and radiating everywhere. Surrounded by the kiss of the ocean, languid beneath that of the stars, Oaleya is sleeping divinely.

With a dull moan, Kouang raises his head. His ears prick, catching a distant purr. It is not a storm. The volcano Hakarou is not angry. What demons are amusing themselves aping the thunder?

The children have woken up too, listening to the rumor. They mutter in unison: "May the passing gods be blessed," but they do not have the strength to raise their palms toward the unknown and fall asleep again.

Similar to the heavy waves that are breaking in the hollows of the cliffs, the distant rumble continues to purr. Is there not a glimmer on the horizon other than that of the stars, the sky or the sea? Houang's chops

41

crease in a grimace of anger. With one of his muscular arms he takes hold of Rara; with the other he grabs Mémé, and he carries them away.

In a few strides he is at the entrance to the grotto, and crosses the threshold. His nostrils are soothed by the familiar odor of seaweed, dry grass and bat guano in the refuge he has chosen. He deposits the two light bodies on the armfuls of wrack and forage that he has piled up. Rara's head lodges itself flirtatiously on Mémé's bosom, where the palpitating creature that she has given to him resides, and Mémé takes possession of Rara's arm, which is hers. Their even respiration is confused with the murmur of eternal life.

Then Kouang goes to sleep too. From time to time, a faint groan escapes his monstrous breast—because Kouang, whether he is asleep or awake, cannot escape the terrible images engraved in his by the horror of his destiny.

For this is the destiny of Kouang...

II. THE STORY OF KOUANG

It is an immense mysterious island where, amid the furnaces of the Equator, the secret reserves of life ferment in inviolate retreats.

In vain has the insatiable curiosity of the white man attempted to penetrate therein. In vain has his need for knowledge, possession and lure precipitated his scientists, his heroes and his pirates therein. He has only been able to erect a few fragile outposts on its shores, where a handful of feverish functionaries wither and quarrel, to push on a few dozen kilometers up the black rivers with the oily waters; to fell a few square leagues of forest; to conclude illusory treaties with the fabulous wooly-haired monarchs with disquieting jaws; to attempt to turn spaces thus far left blank of the maps of geography red or blue. His obstinate perseverance and malevolent ingenuity have scarcely scratched the surface of the mysterious island. The island repels him and defends itself.

Protecting it, there are numerous cannibal tribes. They are armed with assegais and poisoned arrows; their courage is indomitable. Frightful beatitudes are promised to the killers of white men. There are also bloodthirsty wild beasts and infernal reptiles. Here, Nature has sculpted her most ferocious tigers, her most deformed lizards, the entire spectrum of serpents with venomous fangs. There is a pandemonium of voracious spiders, scorpions, centipedes, mosquitoes, giant ants, flies and gnats of every shape and size. They assault humans relentlessly, giving them no truce by day or by night, penetrating into their eyes, their ears, their nostrils, attacking their flesh through boots and garments. Incessantly, humans brush, swallow, breathe in and absorb though every pore an animal population intent on draining their being, eating them away and impregnating them with its poisons.

An inextricable vegetable barrier defends every yard of the forbidden kingdom, foot by foot. Arboreal phalanges whose trunks blunt iron extend over impenetrable thickets of ferns, entangled with creepers, cacti and reeds as dense as fields of wheat and as sharp as spears. Against their compact masses, axes are blunted, sabers break and fire expires, stifled by the suffocating moisture of the atmosphere.

Here and there, at a prodigal cost in lives, humans have been able to force a breach, sketch out a trail. Then, putrid miasmas have sprung from the spongy soil, furious fevers and diseases that hollow out faces, crush brains and empty bellies. Scarcely traced, the paths are strewn with white skeletons, soon swallowed up in the mud beneath lush vegetation. All those who set out to conquer the forest are swallowed up by it, digested and dissolved.

There, it is said, tracked by the ambitious biped, ineradicable Nature has sheltered its final alembic, hidden its ultimate treasures and—who can tell?—concealed obscure and surprising life-forms. Hence the ardor with which, since the first years of the twentieth century, the Fehlenbeck Company of Hamburg has besieged the isle. Wild beasts are a commodity more sought-after every day. There is no Duchy of Gerolstein[8] that does not de-

---

[8] The reference is to a light opera by Jacques Offenbach, *La Grande-Duchesse de Gérolstein* (1867). The eponymous anti-heroine is a tyrant used to having all her whims satisfied; her chamberlain, Baron Puck, starts a war simply to amuse her.

mand them for its zoological garden, no foundation established by a Yankee sub-billionaire that does not claim them for its museum. Prices rise in proportion to the abundance of customers, but the furnishing of tigers and alligators, baboons and hippopotamuses, although it brings in better dividends every day, is also becoming more arduous every day. The reserves of India and Africa are exhausted or decadent. German ingenuity, incapable of manufacturing *ersatz* elephants or orangutans is obliged to pursue the product where it exists.

The Fehlenbeck Company has, therefore, established the largest of its trading posts on the shore of the large island. It has staffed it with an elite personnel, and does not withhold any means of action therefrom. If men die, others come running from the sandy steppes of Brandenburg or the romantic banks of the Rhine to pick up the torch. The tall blonde women of Germany with the robust thighs know their duty, and do not shirk it. For the grandeur of the *Vaterland*, they give birth to the necessary human raw material; German commerce and German science receive the required champions from them.

And if, perhaps, behind the commercial décor and intellectual research, other objectives are hidden; if, around the huts, cages, stables and hangars other constructions are discreetly huddled or hollowed; if, from vessels fitted out for the transportation of animals, every

---

The metaphorical relevance to the present text probably ends there, but it might be worth noting that the Duchess, chastened as a result of her erotic misadventures, eventually formulates a famous line whose approximate translation is "if you can't have the one you love, you might as well love the one you can have."

time they return to the mouth of the Elbe, an entire menacing metalwork is unloaded by night, which is already invisible by morning; if, more directly and even more ambitiously, the trading-post of Wilhemstadt collaborates in the surge of "World Politics", what a surplus of excitement for its personnel!

In appearance, it is a matter of furnishing anatomical specimens or experimental subjects to the laboratories of Dresden or Berlin, of sketching Sundays at the "Zoo" before a horde of marsupial London cockneys and their rosy-cheeked offspring. In reality, it is a matter of ensuring Teutonic emprise over the planet, of tightening the mesh of the net with which it intends to surround the world.

At the head of the operation is Dr. Otto Klagenmeyer. Scarcely forty, robust, thickset, massive and bald-headed, with a scarred and clean-shaven face and gold-rimmed spectacles perched on a fleshy nose, his chin square and jutting, he devotes himself to his task with the studious zeal that attracted attention on the benches of the University of Bonn, the enterprising spirit that subsequently made him peerless among the agents of the company, and the patriotic fervor that reveals the heroic type of the sovereign people whose prerogative is to rule the world.

His outpost is a combat station, a station of conquest. From the millenarian forest he extracts dividends that increase the wealth of the old Hanseatic city, discoveries that raise the prestige of the German University, and elements of strength that add something to imperial glory. The cargoes of wild beasts and snakes, collections of minerals and plants, bottles of insects, mollusks and fish, and notebooks of observations that every ship brings back are as many victories of Teutonic genius. It is not only humankind that he will enslave, it is Nature. She has been able to defend herself so long as humans were only human, but she will succumb to the hegemony of the Nietzschean hero. It is for him to violate her supreme arcana.

Her supreme arcana are those whose enigmas are the most troubling.

It is beyond doubt that the hinterland of the great Island constitutes the most prodigious cauldron of life in the terrestrial crust. Those explorers who have come back from their expeditions have reported bizarre vestiges. In spite of the powerful decomposing effects of the soil, they have collected fragments of bone, pelts and excrements that do not correspond to any known species, living or extinct. Enormous imprints hardened in the mud could not be identified.

It is appropriate to connect these indications with tales long thought to be fantastic that circulate among the aborigines. According to them, extraordinary beings whose forms participate in those of apes and humans live in the impenetrable jungle bordering the marshes of Bang-Tao. Their stature surpasses that of orangutans, their strength that of a bear, their intelligence that of the shrewdest magicians. Hunters claim to have glimpsed them, but that it is futile attempting to catch them. Their cunning is only surpassed by their ferocity. Of all those who have attempted to reach their lairs, nothing more has been heard, or their cadavers have been found with the neck vertebrae crushed, the skulls staved in and the limbs broken.

It would be naïve to base any credence on what the indigenes say. They are more than half-duped themselves by the fables created and incessantly modified by their puerile imagination. Partially corroborated by con-

47

crete evidence, however, the stories are not totally negligible. Is it entirely impossible that, protected by all the forces of equatorial Nature, by marshes, rivers, giant trees, unbreakable lianas, tigers, alligators, venomous insects, poisonous reptiles, quicksands, putrid mud, all the miasmas and all the contagions, a few specimens exist in the depths of the island womb of species vainly sought, or presumed extinct without leaving traces?

Perhaps—who can tell?—one of those primates conjectured by anthropology, logical and thus far ungraspable links between human cave-dwellers and the great apes...

A bold and extravagant hypothesis, certainly. It was even bolder and more extravagant to establish on the sandy heathlands of Brandenburg the basis of the monarchy that will, in future, wear the crown of Europe. Dr. Klagenmeyer has resolved that he will obtain proof of the existence or non-existence of the problematic monster. Such a discovery would be good publicity for the company, an incomparable trophy for German science and would guarantee worldwide celebrity for its maker.

It is in vain, thus far, however, that the most tempting rewards have been offered to the Dayak hunters. The majority have refused, with a superstitious dread. Those who have allowed themselves to take the bait have never returned.

Three expeditions commanded by Europeans have had no more success. Dr. Karl Schmidt, who led the first, was torn to pieces by a tiger, and Hugo Vogt, who accompanied him, died within twenty-four hours of a pernicious fever on the banks of the Guinga.

The second had a more macabre outcome. Karl Müller, having gone mad, murdered his two companions before blowing his own brains out. Dr. Klagenmeyer has kept to himself the incoherent notes of his travel log, brought back by a native guide. Master of his nerves as he is, their horror—the corrosion of that brain, of that human will gradually disintegrated by solvent effluvia—caused him to grind his teeth for several evenings.

Perhaps, had it not been for the youthful impetuosity of Julius Strassberg, fresh out of Tübingen, he would have hesitated to give him the order to depart. He would have been wrong. After three months, the Malay porters, working in shifts, brought back a delirious skeleton on a stretcher, whose bones were breaking through the black, scaly and bloody skin. Before dying, however, Strassberg recovered a few minutes of lucidity. His eyes clear and his words distinct, gripping the hand of his superior in his final spasms, he murmured: "It exists."

Strassberg had penetrated as far as the abode of the prodigious anthropopithecus.[9] He had contemplated with his own eyes a kind of primitive hut, the walls of which were made of bamboo, reeds and twigs, interlaced with a commencement of artistry. A litter of foliage conserved the imprint of two bodies. There were calabashes of different sizes, a couple of gourds, a kind of blanket of woven leaves and rushes: the embryo of a furniture. It was no longer the shelter of an ape. A human, then?

---

[9] The term *anthropopithecus*, originally suggested as a generic label for the chimpanzee, was appropriated by various commentators to describe the "Java man" whose fossil remains were discovered by Eugène Dubois in 1891. Lichtenberger is careful not to name the island on which Klagenmeyer is working or to attribute any identifiable terms to its geography, but he obviously has Java man—widely advertised at the time as Ernst Haeckel's hypothetical "missing link" between humans and apes—in mind in constructing this element of the story.

Julius Strassberg closed and reopened eyes in which life was flickering one last time.

"I saw it prowling under the lataniers. It's not a man. It's…a great Hairy Thing. The one we're searching for. The link… All the details…in my journal… For science and for the Kaiser…send my ring back to Fraülein Frieda, my back-pay to my mother. I hope that the Company will add an extraordinary gratification. Goodnight…"

No hesitation is permissible. Scarcely have Julius Strasberg's remains been buried in the murderous soil than Otto Klagenmeyer has prepared his revenge. For two months, he studies the dead man's documents, assembles weapons, food, clothes, footwear and medicines. Willingly or by force, he obtains the best guides and the most robust porters.

On the appointed day, the imperial flag is hoisted on the roof of the trading-post before the assembled employees. A salvo of cannon-fire salutes him. Dr. Klagenmeyer gives his orders to his deputy, and, in the midst of the personnel's cries of "*Hoch!*" and the prostrations of the indigenes, he takes personal command of the expedition that moves off. If the Great Hairy One exists, Herr Klagenmeyer will bring it back, or will not come back himself.

But he will come back.

In the heart of the maternal forest, Kouang the giant and his companion Koua are placidly stringing out the identical days that the caprice of Nature has been pleased to provide for them.

Beyond the thorny thickets and pestilential pools that surround the great retreat, amid prodigious forests, impenetrable foliage with extravagant fruits, in the ac-

cumulation of reeks and odors, in the bosom of the un-
dergrowth where the kiss of the sun and the decomposed
humus give birth to fantastic flowers, in a dense and vertiginous pullulation of forms, sketches, existences, ago-
nies and putrescence, Kouang is king and Koua is queen.

Their mighty torsos delightedly breathe in the mi-
asma-charged air that makes their blood thicker and their
limbs, as stout a tree-trunks, more muscular. Before
them, the tiger lies down in the grass, its ears flat, and
the stupid rhinoceros turns away. Elephants salute them
amicably with their trunks, and alligators beat a retreat.
One evening, Krawac, the doyen of the long-jawed
brutes, dared to attack the huge couple when they went
down to the river to bathe. With one bound, Kouang
climbed on to his shoulders and clenched his knees, took
hold of his muzzle with both hands, and dislocated the
reptile's crushing apparatus, with frightful cracking
sounds, in a matter of seconds.

Against the hairy pelt of the giants, all vermin are
impotent, including human vermin. One evening, when
their whim had taken them a few leagues from their lair,
swinging from tree to tree, they had encountered a
Dayak hunter. He had fled in fear, after having released
a dart that they had sniffed and palpated disdainfully, as
inoffensive as that of mosquitoes.

In any case, their temperament is peaceful. They
nourish themselves on fruits, herbs, roots and honey. No
ambitious dreams or complicated curiosities are sketched
within their skulls. Their thoughts circulate around the
sun, water, shadows, odors, tastes and sounds. And they
love one another. They love one another delicately and
powerfully. They do not care about anything else. Only
rare reminiscences occasionally pass through them.
Once, other hairy giants roamed the great forest, and it

was appropriate to crouch down together while exchanging clusters of fruit or tubers, but the great siblings have disappeared. Why? Since Kouang has Koua, and since Koua is Kouang's, what does it matter? They love one another...

They love one another. They do not know evil. They do not know fear. They live insouciantly, cradled in immense Nature, known, proven and fraternal.

However, the mistrust subsists within them that permits an individual to endure in the concurrence of instincts and appetites. Meticulously, every morning, at first light, they beat the bush, explore the treetops, and inspect the marsh. It is less to seek provender than to verify that nothing new and nothing strange has insinuated itself therein. Perhaps their memories have retained distant images, disconcerting effluvia, suspicious imprints. Everything known to them is friendly; unknown, everything is suspect, everything potentially hostile...

Everything unknown is suspect—hence, this morning, the troubling apprehension that is tormenting Kouang, extracting hoarse groans from him. For three days, torrential rain has wiped out all tracks and all fumets. In addition to sight, hearing and smell, however, existence in the woods develops in their denizens a special sense, a sharp and distant tactile sense, a prescience of any disturbance in the order of things.

This morning, breaths and rustles are quivering in the jungle, which are in violation of custom. In the foliage, the chatter of parrots has a shrill tone; they are flapping their wings, calling to one another, flying toward the sun. Flattening their trunks and ears, a herd of elephants emerges from the west; they bathe, drink, spread mud on the napes of their necks and resume their march. In the gusts of the heavy breeze that escorts them, are not indefinable warnings floating? In the distance—far in the distance—a rumor is propagating.

Kouang hesitates, grinds his teeth, and grips his club harder. There is a threat. Naïve anger is born in him, and increases, deepening. Who, then, dares...? But beside him, Koua is frolicking, cheerful and charming. She looks at him in surprise and mocks him impishly. He contemplates her, irresolute. No harm must come to her. Perhaps it would be best to flee—but where? Nostrils flared, Kouang sniffs the surroundings. Now Koua also has an intuition of danger, and formulates an anxious interrogation. Kouang grabs her wrist and draws her toward the thicket...

He stops, coughs with rage and strikes his chest...

Three or four sickly beasts with an indescribable odor dare to bar his way, making anxious gestures...

Then, rendered furious, Kouang charges, howling. Thunder, blinding lightning and biting pain fall upon him, stupefying him...

What has happened? Koua, collapsed in the grass at his feet, is exhaling moans. There is the atrocious odor of her streaming blood. In spite of his wounds, Kouang takes hold of one of the hunters in one hand, another in the other, whirls them around, and smashes their skulls against rough tree-trunks, to which their brains adhere. The rest flee.

Kouang picks up the inert Koua, whose eyes are capsizing, and hugs her to him. He will save her from harm. But extraordinary bonds fall over his shoulders, strangling him and entangling his limbs. An infamous horde rushes forward. In vain he struggles, strikes out, bites and runs. Things pierce him, enchain him, and pin him to the ground.

Drunk with pride and wrath, Dr. Klagenmeyer congratulates and scolds his men feverishly. But for their cowardice and precipitation, he would have captured the anthropoid couple alive. No matter; it is a triumphal day. Kouang's wounds are slight; he will recover. In Hamburg, the cyclopean captive will be the star attraction at the Fehlenbeck Park, and will amaze the crowds. The dissection of the female promises the most instructive revelations. Her remains, duly stuffed—a gift from Professor Klagenmeyer—will constitute the jewel of the Berlin Museum.

Back there, in an elegant house in Wilmersdorf, with a Louis XV façade adorned with stucco giraffes and Medieval ironwork, he glimpses a tall blonde maiden with flaxen tresses. Embroidering the initials of her beloved fiancé on the cushions that she is stuffing with her own hair, Lina Wagenroth is quivering with love and pride.

Between the decks of the *Kaiser Wilhelm*, a solid cage is fitted. In the depths of that cage, Kouang is curled up, mulling over the inconceivable catastrophe again and again.

Although his head lodges a brain whose weight—as the dissection of Koua has proved—surpasses that of orangutans by a quarter, and whose circumvolutions approach in complexity those of Hottentots, the sketchy intelligence with which whimsical Nature has endowed him is vacillating in confrontation with the horror of his destiny. In what soul he has, a few images, always the same, collide atrociously and relentlessly.

There is a frightful odor in the maternal forest of his birth.

There are the silhouettes of murderers.

There is the battle, the thunder, the flame, the pain, and the spreading blood of Koua.

There is—the jaws of the captive tremble convulsively—the leader of the murderers, the monster with the eyes that hide and the hairless skull, bending over Koua's corpse, tearing it apart with his claws of steel. There is the scattered flesh of his beloved, her poor bloody remains swaying from the branches of trees.

There is the infernal journey in the moving prison, the arrival among the stinks, the figures, the noises that render him mad.

There are other shocks thereafter, other disgusts, other cruelties, and the embarkation in a hubbub of vertigo on the thing that stirs.

There is the intense nostalgia for the disappeared forest, the bitter anguish of the immense barely-glimpsed sea, the sharp breath of which stings him and gnaws all the way to be bone-marrow.

There is the bewilderment, the desperate need to sleep forever.

Another instinct combats that, however, and overwhelms it, constraining Kouang to absorb the fetid nourishment deposited in his cage. Day and night, Kouang seems to be dozing, with his eyes half-closed, but beneath his lowered eyelids, his pupils are alert. Every time Herr Klagenmeyer comes to prowl around his ape, those eyes light up and watch him. Perhaps, one day, he will come close enough…but the leader with the smooth head distrusts him. Guards armed with iron pikes are charged, on his orders, to keep watch on the captive between the bars.

On a daily basis, notebook in hand, Klagenmeyer spends several hours observing his captive. His jubilation in unparalleled. Following Koua's dissection, no further doubt is possible. It is a scientific coup, the evidential proof of evolutionism. Until now, the distance between the group of apes and humans has remained greater than is usual between family members, almost equivalent to the one separating monkeys from lemurs. This fills in the gap. From primitive protoplasm to superior humankind, from the Moneron[10] to Kant or Wilhelm II, the thread is uninterrupted.

Carefully prepared, Koua's skeleton has been placed in a crate moored in front of Kouang's cage. Aided by his assistant, Franz Metzger, Dr. Klagenmeyer has examined, measured, catalogued and listed its elements minutely. Alongside the skeleton, the study of the living organism completes the verification.

"In truth, Professor, that skull surpasses in capacity those of Fuegians and Tasmanians. I don't know whether my imagination is carrying me away, but I discern a glimmer of hatred in our prisoner's eye that crosses the bounds of animality, attaining consciousness."

Klagenmeyer's square chin acquiesces with his collaborator's words; he gazes with satisfaction at the huddled Kouang, whose eyes never leave him.

---

[10] Like the term "missing link"—and, indeed, closely akin to it—the concept of the Moneron, a hypothetical primal living entity, is due to Ernst Haeckel. Lichtenberger, whose brother was a professor of German literature at the University of Paris, was probably directly acquainted with Haeckel's work, but it is possible, given certain other significant echoes (including the ornithorhynchus) that he has taken some inspiration from Louis Boussenard's Vernian fantasy *Les Secrets de Monsieur Synthèse* (1888; available in a Black Coat Press edition as *Monsieur Synthesis*, ISBN 9781612271613), which is set in the Coral Sea and makes much of Haeckel's evolutionary theories, waxing lyrical on the subject of the Moneron.

"Truly, Metzger, I don't believe that your observation is devoid of foundation, and I can't recommend you too urgently to complete the collection of photographs of our guest. Nevertheless, to any craniological measurement, to the strongest reasoning, to any psychological hypothesis, I prefer that certainty..." He points to a series of small bones lined up in a box on a bed of cotton, and asserts, in a professorial voice: "What distinguishes my captive from all the apes, that which makes him what sciences has sought, is that, alone with humans, he possesses, not four hands but two feet."

With love and with fervor, the professor lifts up the fragments one by one, describes, comments and deduces. The tibio-tarsal mortise only permits rigorous movements of extension and flexion. All the tarsal bones are stout and broad. The axis of the tibia, the vertical axis of the astragalus and the antero-posterior axis of the calcaneum are all in the same plane.

"Look at the thickness of the first toe, almost the same length as the second, parallel to it. The cuneometatarsal articulation is an arthrody that does not permit either adduction or abduction. The sole of the organ is an arch weighing solidly upon the ground at three points. In truth, that foot is a human foot, a masterpiece of adaptation to a vertical stance, exactly contrary to that presented by the pithecoid, cebian or anthropoid apes."

On the orders of the professor, who is sea-sick—it also makes him terribly thick-headed—the steward has brought a bottle of champagne, uncorks it and fills two glasses with the sparkling liquid.

"I invite you, Herr Assistant, to empty this glass with me to the glory of German science and our Emperor."

They rise to their feet and clink glasses: *Prosit!*

With an obsequious chuckle—being on the first rung of his career, he is still going through his servile phase—the assistant draws his master's attention to the captive, whose dull eyes are riveted on them.

"One might think that this French wine is exciting the fellow's curiosity!"

Dr. Klagenmeyer is in a decidedly jovial mood. He ripostes, wittily: "Until now, the Frenchman was the transition between *Homo Germanicus* and the primate. We'll empty our last glass to his equatorial cousin..."

Having drunk, the two men draw away. In the dim light, Kouang's pupils continue to follow them. The odors of the dead Koua, the wine and the tormentors linger in his nostrils. Oh, to squeeze that neck between his fists, to feel it crack! The giant's jaws quiver.

But the torturers have disappeared now; the captive's somber eyes turn away, languidly aimed over the side of the vessel at the horizon. It is striped with singular coppery bands. The atmosphere is suffocating. Going up on to the bridge, the captain exchanges a few clipped remarks with his first mate. Their brows are anxiously furrowed. The barometer has fallen steeply.

Dr. Klagenmeyer approaches. "Well, Commandant, rumor has it that we're going to have a storm?"

The other nods his head. "Perhaps more than that, Doctor."

All night the ship has pitched and rolled. The heavy wooden planks sealing the area between decks have been drawn, the hatches hermetically sealed. In the white dawn, the Kaiser Wilhelm, in battle dress, is fighting grimly against the unleashed elements. It is a typhoon.

All day long, the fury of the sea increases, further aggravated. Mountains rise up, collapse, sweeping the deck. In spite of the valor of the cargo-vessel, a veritable masterpiece of the shipyards of Altona, it is impossible to meet it head on; the vessel changes course and flees, but the hurricane is on her heels, harassing her and shaking her with its titanic rage.

The second night is worse. The whole of the frail ligneous framework strains, oscillates, sinks, rears up, sinks down and groans in pain.

The captain think that it is his duty to warn the doctor: "The ship is under stress, and we're drifting more than we should toward the great subterranean plateau of the Murray Bank."[11]

"Are we in peril?" asked the doctor.

"The situation is serious."

"Very well."

Herr Klagenmeyer makes a parcel of his notes, his photographs, wraps them in a rubber sheet and secures the whole to his chest. In case of shipwreck, these are his orders: firstly, save the ape in the cage, and secondly, the crate containing the skeleton of the other. It is the glory of German science that is at stake. Compared with that, what do a few human lives matter? *Deutschland über alles*.

In the new dawn, the terror is indescribable. In the midst of a dense yellow vapor, in which visibility is lim-

---

[11] The Murray Reef, off the shore of Australia, was a frequent site of shipwrecks in the late nineteenth-century, but the "Murray Bank" featured in the story is an improvisation—similarly named, one presumes, after Sir John Murray (1841-1914), the oceanographer who proposed a theory of coral reef formation in 1880.

ited to ten meters, the vessel in reeling randomly in an apocalyptic swell. Two sailors have been carried away like wisps of straw by a wave. At every movement, shaken to its foundations, one might think that the assemblage of planks and beams were on the brink of falling apart and sinking. The faces of the men are pale with exhaustion; several have blood on their faces or limbs. Supplementary rations of eau-de-vie are scarcely sustaining their energy. In the bosom of the infernal saraband, Dr. Klagenmeyer has not detached himself for a moment from the thought of his conquest. Every two hours he goes into the shadows to inspect his prisoner. Three times a day, in spite of the peril, the ventilation panel is opened briefly.

Clinging to the bars of his cage, Kouang participates, passively, in the unleashing of the horror that surrounds him. He feels neither hunger nor thirst, nor the pain of his bruised flesh, just one obsession: that neck! Oh, his two hands around that plump neck, surmounted by the odious head with the smooth skull: the head whose keen eyes come to insult his misery; the head that reeks of the martyrdom of Koua!

Several times, the fury of the waves has made the walls of his prison creak. The tempests of the sky bring down the proudest giants of the forests; can they not vanquish the magic that confines him?

Kouang noticed on the first day that one portion of that which imprisons him is less immutable than the rest. It is by that route that blows of iron bars chased him into the jail. It closed behind him with a deafening racket. Might it not open again? He has discovered how to move the enormous bolts by putting his hands through the bars; it is only the magic of the lock that surpasses his

Raramémé approaches him or strokes his pelt with their fingers.

On the new land on to which the tide has thrown him, Kouang the Great Hairy One resumes his existence. To be sure, in the thickets of the amiable isle there is not the intensity of germs that impregnated the thick atmosphere of the maternal marshes. There is no longer Koua. He bears painful wounds that will not heal. Sometimes, in the middle of the night, he twitches in pain, howls, and beats the air with his anguished arms. Ineradicable poisons never cease to gnaw at him.

Nevertheless, the sun reanimates the ardor of his blood. He breathes in the salubrious sea-breeze, avidly. The taste of the mangoes and the honey is sweet. The effluvia of the Oyas are of the jungle, and do not inconvenience him. Even so, their form, which reminds him of the violators, is repugnant to him; he avoids them. Only Raramémé, the children of the crab, are in his heart. They have returned his breath to him. Their tiny hands have caressed him.

Their gesture distills a charm from which Koua is not absent. When they go away, the image of the one who has disappeared is blacker. Attenuating the terrible hoarseness of his voice, Kouang has told the children his story. The details are incomprehensible to them, but they perceive the grief in it.

Rara has explained it sufficiently: "A spirit is tormenting the Hairy god. He is hungry for roots and he is thirsty for water, but he has more hunger and more thirst than Raramémé."

The children have adopted the giant's lair; they accompany him in his wanderings, share his pickings and distract him with their games, their dances and their songs.

It is in the order of things, among the Oyas, to associate with beasts and with gods, between whom there is often little difference. Kouang is the Beast-God, the monstrous fetish that the Children of the Crab have chosen. He participates in the consideration that surrounds them.

In the bosom of the peaceful isle, however, Kouang remains prey to the obsessive dream. At the evocation of that which was, and of that which endures, his eyes become bloodshot, his hair bristles. Somewhere on the earth, the enemy with the smooth skull and the plump neck is still breathing...

Patiently, every day, from dawn onwards, Kouang hates Dr. Klagenmeyer, watches out for him, and prowls in his pursuit until nightfall.

Through the mouth of the cave, dawn projects a rosy light. The stalactites of the vault are outlined bizarrely, among which flaccid bats hang down. In the eternally-shadowed fissures, confused movements quiver.

Rara yawns, rubs his eyes with his fists, pushes back his tangled hair. On the other side of the bulky Kouang, whose thorax is swelling up with rhythmic thunder, Mémé is still asleep. It is necessary not to wake her up abruptly. During sleep, her soul sometime wanders for long distances among the spirits. For fear of accidents, she needs time to reintegrate herself with the flesh.

Mischievously, Rara kneels down and, with his elbows on the enormous belly, tickles Mémé's neck and cheeks with the stem of a reed. She pulls a comical face, makes a languid gesture to chase the mosquito away, and finally opens her eyes sulkily.

Rara laughs. She opens her eyes wide, frowns, blows into her cheeks, as if she were malevolent, to scare him, spits and extends her claws like an angry cat. "Ksss...defend yourself!"

On opposite sides of the sleeping colossus, they challenge one another, spitting, bracing themselves, unleashing slaps. Rara is the more adroit at that game. With a swift cuff, he knocks Mémé over. She loses her balance and all of her weight falls on to the monster's face.

Kouang enfolds her in his heavy grip, with a groan. This time, the murderer with the gold-rimmed eyes will not escape him. Mémé struggles, uttering shrieks as shrill as her made laugher will permit. Rara is also laughing too loudly to come to her aid.

The Hairy One squints his dark eyes, catches a momentary glimpse of his aggressors, loosens his grip, sighs and stands up, as he sees them rolling amid the debris of seaweed and forage. Every time they stand up, he knocks them down again more powerfully, carefully moderating the strength of his arms, whose release could stun a rhinoceros.

In the new warmth of the dawn—everything is fresh, everything shines, everything sings, and everything is embalmed—Kouang and Raramémé shake themselves amid the splash of silvery wavelets. As swift in the water as fish, the children clean away the soil of the night and pester the giant. Rara slaps him in the face with a dead octopus. He responds with a cuff that knocks the boy over, swallowed up by water two meters deep. He reappears, breathes out, spits out water and sand, and returns to the assault.

Indigenes of both sexes, holding hands, descend on to the beach, in couples or small groups. They have separated during the night according to the dictates of amour or the signs of blood. At sunrise, the tribal instinct draws them together again. An Oya only enjoys the plenitude of his means when he is with his fellows. Even the boldest hunters do not like to remain away from the village for more than twenty-four hours.

It is not only the fear of prowling demons that torments them but the anguish of isolation. Each of them needs them all, so they scarcely ever go away except in groups of two, three or four, and their custom is to walk with their little fingers linked, and to sleep side by side. Evil can easily overtake the solitary. In the assembled tribe there is wisdom, strength and security.

There are no complicated laws among the Oyas. The forest furnishes them with enough game and roots, the sea enough fish and mollusks, for them to be free of the necessity of labor. They know how to extract fire from stones, which they maintain in order, if they wish, to cook food, and to light the bonfires in the evening around which dancing takes place. The climate is so mild that a few huts of interwoven branches, or the cover of a mulberry bush, constitute sufficient nocturnal shelter. Mores are gentle; children are raised communally; every adult is the father or mother of them all.

Even so, according to the signs that are engraved on their breasts, the Oyas are divided into several clans. All of them, according to whether they are of the armadillo or the kiwi, the sea-urchin or the seagull, associate preferentially with those of their own totem. Quarrels sometimes arise, especially in spring, over rivalries in love, or lack of respect, or incongruous greed. It is appropriate that no Oya eats the beast of his totem, and every Oya, before killing, apologizes for the liberty that he is taking if the victim is the totem of one of his kin.

From the failure to observe rites and customs, disputes can easily arise. Usually, they settle down of their own accord, for the humor of Oyas does not persist for long in a single preoccupation. In cases of bitter conflict, the soul of the tribe is expressed through the words of the elders—Manga-Yaponi is the most venerable—which find a natural echo in all hearts.

Only the people of the octopus sometimes jib against his decisions. Mao exhibits a blameworthy disposition. He and his kin affect to confiscate for their own usage the calabashes from which they eat or the mats on which they sleep. They are irregular in their attendance at the evening assemblies and associate themselves with the traditional hymns without fervor. When the sages have spoken, even though neither the number of his years nor the nobility of his totem qualifies him to do so, Mao sometimes raises his voice and makes speeches that testify to his individualistic tendencies.

Such things did not happen once, but today, respect is waning. So who can be astonished if the anger of the gods is manifest more frequently? It is to be feared that it might end up descending in a catastrophic manner.

At the morning bath, there is little evil to be feared from them, for they have exhausted their malice during the night. Anyway, it is not a time when it is appropriate to be at odds with one another, so dances and hymns are mingled with joyful words, frolics and jesting challenges, and splashing and diving, which are forms of prayer as well as amusement.

When they emerge from bathing they sit down on the sand, and while nimble fingers tear pat nuts or fruits of the sea, assemble seeds or shells with which to make necklaces, or braid garlands of flowers, the elders intone the liturgical chants and the tribe takes up the refrains and responses in chorus.

There is the song of creation.

There is the song of the black flower.

There is the song of totems. Naturally, each clan has property in its own.

There are several songs to appease the dead.

There is one to bless the new-borns.

There is the song of thunder, that of the oceans and that of the sun.

That of the moon is less beautiful, for the sun might be jealous.

There are many others. They are handed down from generation to generation. They subsist, carefully gripped in the memory of the elders. That is the historical, philosophical and moral treasure of the tribe. It is good that everyone should aliment themselves with it throughout the day, whenever there is an opportunity; communal singing is most effective in the morning and the evening.

The songs are sacred, and correspond to the needs of hearts as well as to the tactical counsels of prudence. Raraméme possess for themselves the song of the crab, which comes to them directly from Rahuo, the great crab. They associate themselves piously with all the other canticles, but there is one in particular that they prefer; that is the one that proclaims the veneration of the Oyas for the white gods.

So, when Manga-Yaponi intones it, swaying his white-haired head rhythmically, they come out of the water and sit down near him, filling their ears with the liturgical words. Fervently, they listen to the old man recounting the redoubtable legend.

The events the legend records might date from the time when Rahuo extracted Rahuo from the soft Entity, or might have been witnessed by the ancient, or even the adults of the tribe—who can tell? In the naïve memory of the Oyas, today sinks like a stone in water; memories of prehistory and those of yesterday are rapidly confused, and soon present themselves on the same plane.

The white gods are the privileged of Rahuo. Their arrivals undoubtedly mark great perturbations. The Oyas submit to them meekly. When the pale faces emerged from the waters for the first time, they were appropriately adored, and the great livid ancestor has not been forgotten. As for the magical sign that was erected, it has always been nourished with blue and red.

At the top of their voices, Raramémé sing the refrain with the tribe:

> Fear the livid gods who bring dismay
> The water spat them out and took them away.
> They will come back from the distant blue;
> Where their feet have trod, the earth is taboo.

Then the children fall silent. Eyes fixed, Mémé remains motionless. An anxious expectation parts her lips. Rara squeezes the little girl's right hand with his left hand. "I can feel your heart hurting, Mémé."

"Will they come back?" she stammers.

But they shiver. A murmur passed through the tribe. All their brown index-fingers are pointing toward the sky.

In the pearly blue firmament, something is rapidly increasing in size. It is not a seagull. It is not a great condor or an albatross. The fantastic bird that was glimpsed yesterday evening and is now coming back is more gigantic. Its golden plumage sparkles in the sun's rays; its respiration is that of a monstrous bee with petty thunder in its belly.

Whatever it is, wherever it comes from, whatever its purpose might be, it is a god. Perhaps, in the past, the Oyas did not adore it sufficiently, and that is why anger is rumbling within it. What is it bringing from the regions of mystery where the whim of Rahuo dwells?

The indigenes raise their worshipful hands toward the seaplane, prostrating themselves—and they sing the propitiatory conjuration in chorus, until the moment when, having circled around and gained altitude again, it has disappeared.

III. THE STINKING GODS

Furious demons are kneading and driving black masses of clouds through the sky, beating, howling and biting, uprooting trees, and hurling waves to assault the isle. Yesterday, they were captives in the secret caves and in the hollows of great seashells, where the ear can hear them growling. But Mawi, who is in charge of guarding them, had probably got drunk on fermented palm-juice.

At any rate, presages have announced the catastrophe. Manga-Yaponi was not mistaken about them. Three days ago the setting sun was jaundiced, visibly ill. There were also the dull rumbles of thunder and the unexpected visit of the buzzing bird. Perhaps it has laid an egg full of evil spells somewhere, which have hatched out and released their nuisance into the air.

Such is the violence of the cyclone that the most robust of the Oyas cannot stand up on the shore. They remain buried, pitifully, in the depths of their huts, under the cover of the great groaning trees, muttering litanies. From time to time, the most valiant put spiral conches to their lips and draw bellowing notes therefrom. Perhaps that will frighten the demons and the sun, encouraged, will recover the strength to climb the sky.

Rara and Mémé have taken refuge with the Hairy One in the grotto with the reek of algae and bats. Standing near the threshold, Rara insults the screeching winds and throws stones at them. Mémé admires his bravery and keeps him supplied with projectiles.

Beside them, Kouang dozes. From time to time he opens a pensive eye. At the roaring of the cyclone, images buried within him emerge from limbo. It was amid such turbulence that, as a captive on the moving thing, he broke his irons, came back into the light, saw the accursed face for the last time, and was hurled into the abyss, without being able to close his fists around the plump neck, or break the shiny skull with his iron club.

He utters a plaint that echoes beneath the shadowy vault, and goes back to sleep.

For three months the indefatigable *U-37A* has been pursuing its Polynesian campaign, marauding around the luminous atolls, attacking transport-ships loaded with soldiers, livestock or cereals with torpedoes or cannon-fire, and disappearing as soon as its crime is consummated. In all the secret depots prepared in advance, it has found new provisions. Everywhere, gorged on gold, traitors have kept their word better than honest men. Thanks to her, sixty thousand tons—perhaps eighty thousand—of the enemy fleet have been swallowed up by the phosphorescent waters, among the frightened sharks, to rest forever in cemeteries of coral. *U-37A* has equaled the exploits of the *Emden* and avenged her.[12]

For eighteen months the Allies have been encircling isolated Germany, claiming to have stifled her with their blockade. Germany laughs at their threats, breaking through the overly fragile ring with ease, hoisting the flag of the Kaiser at the antipodes, sowing ruin and death

---

[12] The light cruiser *SMS Emden*, the first of three ships to bear that name, harried Allied shipping in the Indian Ocean in the early months of the Great War, sinking two allied warships and numerous merchant vessels before being run aground after engaging the Australian cruiser *HMAS Sydney* in the so-called Battle of Cocos in November 1914.

among those who believe themselves most effectively sheltered from reprisals. In vain the Japanese, Australian and New Zealand navies, and the few rusty old tubs that French vanity maintains in the Pacific have pursued her, searching the seas, the gulfs, the straits, interrogating, advertising and shouting themselves hoarse. Every time the net seems to be closing upon her, the pirate slips away or breaks through, and manifests herself miles away by a new attack.

The other day, however, she was imprudent. Discovered by the seaplanes of the *Sydney*, wisdom commanded her to play dead or run away. When the periscope revealed a heavily-laden four-master three miles to port, however, Captain Bartsch could not contain himself. His predatory instinct held sway over prudence. Not only did he torpedo his prey, but he lingered in order to sniff around the wreckage, to plunder cases of champagne and barrels of spirits. That is why the submarine was taken by surprise by a French light cruiser, hastening in response to the wrecked vessel's last call for help. Suddenly emerging from behind the headland that had masked it, she had caught the Boche unexpectedly beneath her guns. Two well-aimed shells had cracked several bulwarks and smashed its rudder, preventing any further immersion. If the hunter had not been so lame, it would have been the end of the bird of prey, but the U-boat's speed, superior on the surface, and permitted her to outdistance the adversary, and nightfall had ensured her salvation.

A precarious salvation. Twenty kilometers from her nearest base, deprived of both its best means of defense and its best means of attack, the *U-37A* could no longer count on a long career. At any rate, she would carry out her mission of carnage until the end. She sent an American yacht and a Japanese schooner to the bottom. However, watching the latter sink, and the little yellow men struggling in the swelling sea, Captain Bartsch shakes his bony head, grips the massive shoulder of his fellow officer and sniggers: "Rinse your eyes one more time, Doctor, as our foreign friends say, for, either I'm much mistaken, or this the final exploit of our blessed campaign."

Dr. Klagenmeyer, who, for the past five years, has combined the official functions confided to him by the Fehlenbeck Company with those of the secret organizer of German espionage in Polynesia, is the true leader of the expedition. Although Captain Bartsch commands the ship, the Doctor is the one who issues the directives.

His iron-gray eyes scan the horizon. "In truth, Captain," he says, "I don't think that the Emperor can hope for anything more from us, but I'm searching in vain for the Maori destroyer or the ironclad loaded with riff-raff that will purchase the honor—for we'll make her pay dearly for it, won't we?—of sending us to feed the crabs."

Captain Bartsch laughs louder. "That honor, Doctor, will not be given to men. It's the Devil who will claim it on Hell's behalf." Indicating the sky, striated with coppery clouds, he goes on: "You've had too much experience of these regions not to recognize the precursory symptoms of a typhoon. Although this carcass can withstand anything at a depth of twenty meters, on the surface and crippled we're at the mercy of a gust of wind. If you have a soul, Doctor, think of its salvation, for there's scarcely any doubt, now, that we're going to nourish the blind pale fauna that interests His Highness the Prince of Monaco,[13] or leave our bones on one of the reefs of the Murray Bank.

The Murray Bank! That name…those livid clouds…is this, then, the determined return of an obstinate fatality? The doctor's jaws clench. He replies: "If I were superstitious, Captain, I'd have asked you to commit murder elsewhere. This place is unhealthy for me. It's here that the Fehlenbeck Company's *Kaiser Wilhelm* was lost, along with her cargo, a year before the war. A Norwegian whaler picked me up, with four men—but the waves swallowed up a discovery that would have immortalized my name."

"Oh well," the other croaks, "the time has come to go and look for it. Here comes the dance!"

With a howl that plunges from the sky and races from every horizon, the tempest pounces upon the ship. All night long she struggles. In the morning she is doomed. In the midst of the spray, between the gulfs, the heads of corals are blackening. A few hundred meters away, an indecisive coast is discernible in the mist.

"We're in the middle of the Murray Bank. The shoe has already stamped twice. Twenty seconds from now, we'll shatter like an eggshell."

The captain has put on his dress uniform. Save for the dead, the entire crew is clinging to the deck.

"My friends, we have done our duty. One more '*Hoch!*' for the Kaiser and the old fatherland, and then it's every man for himself."

---

[13] Albert I of Monaco (1848-1922) developed a keen interest in oceanography and palaeontology, and made a significant contribution to the former science in the latter decades of the 19th century.

The enormous shoulder of the roaring sea lifts up the sheet-metal cigar and drops it, heavily. There is a terrible crash. The submarine, snapped in two at a stroke, seesaws on the coral reef, scattering the creatures and things that it contains. Back home, on the banks of the Elbe and the Weser, a few more mothers will not see their sons again, a few more wives are widowed. A few widows of Armorica or Cornwall and a few Basque and Nipponese husbands are avenged.

That night, Rahuo's wrath disregards the most fervent prayers and the most tempting conjurations. In vain, the evil spirits that haunt certain great shells are skillfully extracted and masticated, and in vain they are precipitated into the flames to be burned. In vain, the sharkskin drums are beaten by indefatigable musicians attempting to come to the aid of the stars. One might think that even the sacred fire is repelled by the gifts that are offered to it, licking them with disdain and succumbing to the fury of the demons. Undoubtedly, the return of Atua, the vast night, who existed before Rahuo had the whim of creating existence, is nigh. That the Oyas should return to the Great Artisan the breath that they have received is in order, but it is appropriate that they should exhaust all stratagems before the end.

Perhaps the spirits enclosed in amulets, in hollow nutshells, in kneaded balls, which coppery hands are casting into the fires are too weak to raise themselves up through the seven havens. Perhaps Rahuo is demanding a more considerable offering. Although human sacrifices have fallen into disuse, the tradition subsists. They constitute the supreme recourse in a paroxysm of distress.

It is not only the insidious rancor of the octopus, but an instinct in conformity with principles, to which Mao is obedient in formulating a suggestion: "Rahuo is irritated. Rahuo is the great crab. Let the children of the crab go to converse with the ancestor."

Manga-Yaponi shakes his white head severely. What right has Mao to interfere? Does he know things? How, in a cyclone, can the spirits of children have the strength to brave the unleashed elements and reach the ear of the god? Only the intrepid soul of a hunter in the prime of life, who might attempt the adventure of his own free will, could possibly succeed. If there is one such, let him come forward.

The old man's gaze settles on Mao the indiscreet, who goes pale, stammers and steps back. But here is Tupu-Haré, who presents himself resolutely. For two moons the spirit of Toina, his companion, has been calling to him. She succumbed to the assaults of Rongo-mai, who gnawed at her breast. Tupu-Haré will carry to Rahuo the prayer of his children, and perhaps Rahuo, appeased, will permit him to join what remains of Toina somewhere. In passing, he will encourage the sun to climb back into the sky.

Thus it shall be. Over Tupu-Haré's head, crowned with gardenias, the old man extends his simian paw. He murmurs in a whisper the words he is required to repeat. The other makes a sign to indicate that he has understood. The sage makes a gesture.

His skull shattered by a single blow from a club, Tupu-Haré collapses. Still warm, his body is immediately torn apart and thrown, one fragment at a time, into the fire. The flames deign to welcome him, consuming him and crackling with an ardor that is a good omen.

Indeed, the furious souls of the winds are softening now, and calming down. Drawn in Tupu-Haré's wake, they have quit the fortunate isle, rising up with him toward the radiant solitude, where Rahuo, curled up, is delighting in his own perfection.

In the morning, with noisy cries of joy, the Oyas bound out of their huts and shelters, extending the homage of their coppery palms toward the refreshed sun. Once more the old sage has been able to appease the wrath of the gods. His prestige is further increased by that success.

Like the birds—which, now the downpour has passed, are smoothing their foliage and making merry in the purified atmosphere—the Oyas disperse, picking up coconuts, mangos and oranges and unearthing the bulbs of ferns and manioc. Soon, the hunters set off in search of more substantial fare. The fruits and roots will suffice to calm the initial hunger. Warmed up by the warmth of the star, men, women and children crack mollusks between their teeth and shell nuts.

Pecking in the same way, in the thickets of guavas and mulberries, are a thousand beaks of multicolored birds, which only pause in order to exchange strident calls. Suddenly, however, they fly away with shrill clamors. A band of monkeys has arrived to disturb the feast.

Similarly, as if at a given signal, the Oyas interrupt their feast. Only a few bronze children continue to fill their rounding bellies. One by one, or in couples, the adults flow back toward the elders, listening gravely to the revelations that fall from the lip of Tereko.

Tereko wanted to chase away his hunger with oysters. A little while ago, he went to the beach, and there, on the strand, a prodigious spectacle has struck his eyes. Like very pale men, a group of gods has emerged from the water, and hoarse groans are emerging from their lips.

At this redoubtable news, hands seek one another out and clasp one another. The women begin whimpering. All faces turn toward the elders in whom wisdom resides.

Tereko is a child of the armadillo. He is in possession of his reason. His tongue does not assemble words at random. Might he not be the victim of an illusion, though? In order that his words might be verified and that everyone should give further thought to them, he repeats his deposition, and then repeats it again. The terms are identical, but further details are added. The unknown gods are as numerous as the fingers of a hand. Near them, on the shore, all kinds of debris have been washed ashore. The sounds they are making are emerging from the nose and the throat. A terrifying odor emanates from them.

Humans live night and day in the midst of spirits. The latter include visible ones and invisible ones. They are resident in the waters, under stones, in the trees, in animals, and in human bodies themselves. In addition to drinking, eating and sleeping, and before love, the greatest concern of the Oyas is to capture their benevolence, or, at least, to ward off their hostility. The evil that they might do is far superior to the good that can be expected of them. The arrival of the new gods is, therefore, not a very extraordinary event in itself, but it is surely calamitous.

Fragments of old tales rise up in memories. Several times before, the white divinities have emerged from the sea. Perhaps a few of the elders should contemplate their faces. They know what can be done to placate them.

From the lips of Manga-Yaponi, who has just manifested his sagacity in such a decisive manner, the Oyas await the precepts that will dictate their conduct. To be sure, fear is making their hearts beat faster, but also an infantile curiosity. Good is never entirely good, nor evil entirely bad. There were white gods accompanied by thunder, from which a dazzling death flowed, but they possessed in bizarre seashells a bitter and delightful beverage that gave forgetfulness and magical dreams.

To aid him, Manga-Yaponi has summoned old Haoré and also Kupu. They hold council, watching the images rise within them that this adventure suggests to them, comparing them—and sending away Mao, who, as usual, tries to intrude his worries into their august deliberations.

After a time, they get up. "Listen!"

In the midst of his attentive people, Manga-Yaponi formulates the oracle. Everyone gathers together, and, with the elders at the head, the entire tribe sets off. On the way, they ornament their hair and necks with garlands of flowers. Women collect bananas, guavas and mangoes in banana-leaves.

The shipwreck is complete. Of the valiant submarine *U-37A*, the pride of the imperial navy, nothing remains but a few formless items of wreckage dispersed over the shore, and those that the sea is continuing to wash up.

The entire crew has perished, with the exception of the five unfortunates who, as dawn succeeds the night of the disaster, have got to their feet and gathered together. Cadet Waldmann and Seaman Klein, carried to shore together, found Sub-Engineer Schwartz half a mile away, who had just recovered his senses and was bandaging his broken arm as best he could. They have been joined by Seaman Freiguth, whose scratches are benign. And among the half-dozen more or less mutilated bodies that they have identified, over which the vermin of the sea are already swarming, they have succeeded in reanimating—with what joy and veneration!—that of Doctor Otto Klagenmeyer. His presence cheers them up, but, bruised and weak, with no weapons and no food, and their clothes in tatters, what hope is there for them on this hostile coast?

Dr. Klagenmeyer has swallowed a few handfuls of mollusks, and cracked the carapaces of a dozen crabs between his teeth. Thus restored, he has recovered enough lucidity to take stock of the situation. And while the sailors continue to collect mollusks and crustaceans, he formulates his conjectures to Herr Waldmann.

In fifteen hours of the typhoon, *U-37A*, without a rudder, has been driven completely off course. It is impossible to estimate in a precise fashion where they have landed, although it is surely on one of the reefs of the Murray Bank, the immense coralline plateau from which occasional atolls project, theoretically possessed by England or France, but whose approaches are carefully avoided by mariners because of the still-general ignorance of its rare and shallow passes.

It is one of those points of the globe that nature has defended most ferociously against the curiosity of the white man celebrated by Kipling. If Germany had planted her flag there, the secret would doubtless have been forced out long ago, but it is doubtful that any English or French navigator has ever set his footballer's or absinthe-drinker's foot on this island. If it is inhabited, it is by aborigines reduced to the lowest degree of humanity.

"It's necessary for us to expect the worst treatment, then?" asks Herr Waldmann.

"Including being roasted and eaten—for a substantial part of the domain held by the champions of civilization against Teutonic barbarity is still populated, in Oceania as in Africa, by cannibals. Nevertheless, some of these savages have maintained in their mores the forbearance that tenderized Cook's Biblical Puritanism and unleashed Bougainville's humanitarian verbosity in the eighteenth century."

"In any case, Doctor, we'll soon find out."

At the edge of the coconut grove, a few silhouettes are outlined. Other figures are emerging and advancing.

The frightened sailors gather around their leader. Dr. Klagenmeyer stiffens, and proffers, in a commanding voice: "We've been discovered. Flight is futile. Stand firm."

Arms folded, his gaze haughty, he advances to meet the elder Manga-Yaponi.

At his approach, all the heads crowned with flowers bow down. The coppery hands offer their palms. Getting up again, the sage sketches a kind of entrechat and articulates:

"Blessed be the gods emerged from the sea. May their anger spare the Oyas. Ten years ago, and ten years more and other tens of years yet, when I was a young and robust man and the spirits of these people were still wandering in the woods, gods similar to you in the color of their faces—but their emanation, O divinity was far less fetid—similarly deigned to emerge from the waves. They set foot on this land, manifested their power by drawing thunderbolts from their hands and making us drink maddening and exquisite liquors. On that mountain"—the old man's finger pointed to the bluff where, at the top of a mast, the taboo rag was fluttering—"they planted their totem. Under threat of the most frightful punishments, they commanded us to honor it, and then they went back to the whaling-pirogue that had vomited them forth. They surrounded themselves with thunder before our wonderstruck eyes and drew away majestically, probably returning to be swallowed up by the great soft Entity from which Raduo extracted Oaleya.

"Divinites, we have scrupulously followed your orders. As the evil spirits of the rain ate away your totem we have repaired it from time to time; we have carefully nurtured the red with the blood of the turtle-dove and the blue with the blue clay that our women knead and mix with oil in calabashes. Thus, redoubtable god, you are at home here. We are honored by your visit. We extend to you our arms laden with fruit and roots. If you desire fish and game, our hunters will bring them to you. If you desire amour, there are our wives. And if the bloodshed of any of us is agreeable to you, you have only to command.

> The gods are strong, the gods are beautiful
> We prostrate ourselves at their feet
> The gods are strong, the gods are beautiful
> When they speak, we obey, and are complete."

When the Sage has spoken, all heads bow immediately, hands implore, and with a single voice, the tribe modulates the propitiatory hymn.

Of the old ape's jargon, naturally, Herr Otto does not understand a word, but there is no doubt as to the benevolent attitude of the unfortunates. It is a matter of exploiting it—and to begin with, of eating.

Dr. Klagenmeyer puts his index finger to his lips in a majestic manner, clicks his tongue and belches, in a thunderous voice: "*Essen!*"

The divine verb is understood. Overcoming their sacred terror, the women pile up juicy berries and succulent roots before the castaways. The doctor and his companions swallow them avidly, without ceasing to overwhelm the indigenes with their gazes, which become more imperious as their hosts reveal themselves to be more inoffensive.

With enthusiastic approval, the Oyas salute the magnificent appetite of the fortunate, while the doctor whispers to Waldmann, making him party to a hope that has entered into him: "Herr Ensign, it's possible that we're saved. Prepare to become a god."

While guzzling, his resolute mind ripens a plan.

"First, it's important to reconnoiter. We'll have ourselves guided to the observatory that the mummy pointed out to us just now."

Klagenmeyer places his heavy hand on the old man's quivering shoulder. He points to the cliff. "Up there! *Vorwaerts!*" And as the elder seems to hesitate momentarily, he shakes him hard enough to dislodge his last remaining teeth and make his eyes bulge. "*Schnell!* Right away!"

The order is grasped. Because of their singular color and the terrible odor they exhale, the savages dare not get too close to the livid gods, but they nod their heads, clap their hands, brush their mouths with their fingers and then extend them toward the totem of the heights. And then, making a sign to the visitors to follow them, they set forth.

At the edge of the coconut grove, Waldmann hesitates. "You have no fear of an ambush?"

Klagenmeyer shrugs his shoulders. "By the Devil's grace! Don't fail to pick up a few clubs on the way. It's a matter of making an impression on these fellows and, to begin with, taking possession of this land in the name of our glorious Emperor."

In spite of the terrible voices croaking in their throats, the gods do not seem to be irritated. They are largely satiated and have not demanded any sanguinary sacrifice. In the underwood, the tribe capers around them joyfully. While frightened kangaroos and macaques flee, the castaways pause to collect a few clubs. Docile to their desire, the savages hasten to their aid, fashioning them. At each thicket the women gather guavas and mangoes, offering them timidly. Having eaten their fill, the sailors refuse them. But the she-apes are not so very repulsive; Freiguth grabs one by the arm and pulls her toward him. She pales in terror, but allows herself to be drawn.

The doctor, perceiving the action, howls: "Let go! A fortnight in irons to the first man who approaches one of these sluts."

For an hour they make their way through the tree-ferns and giant acacias. Marvelous butterflies and flow-er-birds take off from all the embalmed bushes. Nature lavishes all the grace of her landscapes, the sparkle of her brightest colors and the caress of her most delicate hues on the newcomers. She envelopes them with an immense seductive kiss.

Covetously, Dr. Klagenmeyer articulates: "This land seems blessed by the Lord. It's scandalous that such resources remain fallow. The imminent triumph of Germany will ensure a more rational exploitation of the globe.

The curtain of trees brightens. They emerge into shorter and sparser brushwood. Here is the cliff. To the right there is the sheen of the ocean, the majesty of the smoke-crowned volcano. To the left palpitates the soft iridescent swell of the fortunate isle. An exceedingly soft murmur is comprised by the singing of all the birds and the buzzing of all the insects. The breeze is heavy with all perfumes.

"Tarteiffle!"[14] bellows Klagenmeyer.

His eyes are bulging. With his forefinger he indicates the mast erected on the bluff that overlooks the sea. Until now, his myopic eyes deprived of spectacles have not suspected the scandal. Now that they are at the foot of the mast there is no more doubt. Although its colors are ludicrously distributed, that duster is definitely intended to represent a French flag. The insolent nation whose provocations have constrained peaceful Germany to take up the sword is claiming this Oceanian pearl as one of the links in the excessively heavy necklace under which the skinny shoulders of the slut in question are sagging.

In a vibrant voice, the doctor commands: "Take that down!"

Formidable is the accent of the god. Enthusiastic will be the obedience.

At the foot of the sacred mark that he is indicating for their veneration, the Oyas prostrate themselves, face down. Then, getting to their feet, the young people of both sexes surround the totem with a liturgical round-dance. And in a cheerfully-modulated chorus, they testify their deference:

Honor to the gods, jealous and paternal!
Blessed their taboo, great and eternal!

---

[14] *Tarteiffle* [sic] is an Alsatian curse—a corruption of "Der Teufel" [The Devil]—used with sufficient frequency in 19th-century French drama to be familiar in Paris, although it is slightly surprising to hear Klagenmeyer employing it.

The professor's plump cheeks turn crimson. Is this derision? He elbows his way the ingenuous dancers, falls upon the accursed emblem, swearing, takes hold of the mast and shakes it furiously.

There is a shiver of amazement. Any bizarrerie is permissible to the gods, since they are the gods, but if their desires are contradictory, one has to side with the strongest. Since time immemorial, the trophy on the cliff has been untouchable. It cannot he brought down without terrible punishments descending. The white god is undoubtedly fetid and animated by a redoubtable ardor, but has he measured the consequences of his own action?

A cry of prudence and desolation escapes. The interpreter of his race, Manga-Yaponi brushes the angry arm with his thin fingers and intercedes.

"Superb god, beware of allowing yourself to be carried away by anger. Remember that this sign was commanded to our respect by other divinities that preceded you. Ancient things are doubly venerable. Beware of attracting reprisals upon yourself, and upon us, from which even your vigor might not save you."

If Klagenmeyer were fully in possession of his composure, perhaps he would moderate his fury. If he were to notice, at the present moment, a monstrous silhouette approaching, framed by two slender bronze figures, who is parting the ranks of the savages, sniffing, his rage would doubtless give way to another sentiment—but it is blind, choking. The honor of Germany is at stake. Since these people are begging, he has only to strike hard.

The doctor turns to his sailors and shouts: "Get that rag down!"

As Manga-Yaponi attempts once again to retain him with his long tremulous hands, Klagenmeyer pulls himself free with a blasphemy and punches the old man full in the face with his massive fist, causing the prophet to vacillate and swivel, his nose bloodied, and collapse abruptly, like a dead mollusk.

There is a murmur of consternation among the Oyas. Placid as their temperament is, the instinct of the race would precipitate them to the aid of the man who incarnates it—but their traditional submission to divine will paralyzes them. They hesitate.

Around their leader, the German sailors form up, twirling their clubs.

In the face of the enemy's disarray, Dr. Klagenmeyer feels his strength multiply tenfold. He seethes: "If one of those brutes moves, hit him hard. And you, Freiguth, climb..."

What is it?

The doctor's voice dies in his throat. Livid patches marble the scarlet of his cheeks. He takes a step back, hiccupping: "*Mein Gott!* I'm not dreaming! It's really him!"

They will be the doctor's last words. Kouang's eyes have lit up. With a frightful growl, he pounces. Under his shove, the sailors go down like skittles.

The neck! Two iron fists grip the apoplectic neck...

Koua's murderer struggles, chokes, turns violet...

All the Boches rush to the rescue, but the Great Hairy One's action has freed the collective soul that was in suspense. It is sufficient for one buffalo to stand up to a tiger for the entire herd to charge. The Great Hairy One is also a god sprung from the waters. The children of the crab have adopted him. Manga-Yaponi's spilled blood is crying out for vengeance. Adored for generations, the

tricolor sign is flapping gaily in the breeze, while its pro-
faner is dying on the ground.

The castaways' clubs whirl in vain. A dozen clawed
hands descend upon each of them, which strangle them,
pluck out their eyes, or rip open their bellies. There is a
frightful brawl, which only lasts a matter of seconds.

Everything is concluded.

Five frightfully mutilated bodies lie beside the mast.
Raramémé lift up and drop the inert limbs, curiously.

Kouang is still leaning over Dr. Klagenmeyer's
body. He sniffs it avidly, feels it, contemplates it at
length.

It really is him. It is his face, his neck, his odor.
Back there, in the natal forest...the murder...blood for
blood...

The death of Koua is not causing him so much pain.

Drunk with vengeance, Kouang stands up, parades
a troubled gaze around him, and draws away, awkwardly, with his limping gait.

Rara strikes the cadaver one last time with his harpoon. "The Great Hairy One is a powerful god." And
with Mémé bounding alongside him, they both catch up
with their friend, plunging with him into the green swell,
which closes upon them.

On the battlefield, the tribe remains perplexed. The
surge of atavistic rage having passed, a great deal of unease has resulted from that act of violence. It is not good
to kill. Between the Oyas, quarrels are rare. There are
very few murders others than those solicited by the victims. Even animals are not immolated, except to dispel
hunger. Apologize to those you kill, for everything that
dies exhales dangerous spirits that lie in wait for humans
and which, penetrating into them, engender suffering,
malady, madness and death.

From massacred divinities, extremely noxious effluvia are undoubtedly disengaged. It is urgent and indispensable to ward them off—but how? The embarrassment is cruel, all the more so because Manga-Yaponi, in whom all wisdom resides, is still lying face down in the grass. They turn him over. A feeble breath is still straying over his lips, but his spirit is absent.

So long as he is breathing, no one is qualified to give an order. He is the precious thread that links the past to the present. For want of him, all the treasure of experience scatters like the beads of a broken necklace. Nothing arises in obscure intelligences but confused suggestions. Tongues stammer, impotently.

For want of anything better, gazes turn to old Haoré. Is he not capable of extracting an opinion from his long experience, of capturing the subtle advice of some marauding demon?

He shakes his fleshless head, spits, closes his eyes, mutters. Finally, his trembling lips enunciate a principle that floats up from the ancestral night. Whoever eats the body of a man he has killed assimilates not only his flesh but his spirit. He acquires his virtues and does not risk being importuned by his soul, since he has swallowed it.

That axiom is welcomed in silence and projected in melancholy. Once, yes, they piously masticated the meat of old men. A respectable custom, but it was not pleasant; it has been abandoned. Today, it offends delicacies—and the unbearable stink that the vanquished men give off renders the prospect of the feast particularly unattractive. Even Pahoa and Mohimé, the two gluttons of the tribe, each capable of swallowing a medium-sized kangaroo in a single meal, feel sick. Visions of frightful indigestion afflict the most robustly courageous.

But every authorized speech falls into consciousness like a stone in water, engendering ripples. Clockwork movements are released and engaged, spreading from neighbor to neighbor. Painful as the envisaged gala might be, by virtue of having been formulated, it will become an obsession, an unavoidable necessity.

Fortunately, among the people of the octopus, tradition does not speak as loudly as among those of other totems. Mao often finds fault with the most firmly-established principles. Usually, Manga-Yaponi refutes his sophisms easily, but Mao benefits in this instance from the sage's sealed lips. He also benefits from the disgust that is aroused in all stomachs by the doctrine Haoré has enunciated.

In the general disarray, Mao recalls acrimoniously that not all spirits are good to absorb. Some dry out the chest, others swell the belly, others empty the brain. By what sign has Haoré discerned that those of the white gods are not one of those varieties?

Disconcerted by this objection Haoré shakes his head and mutters. His tongue, not being agile, lacks the magic words.

Triumphantly, Mao redoubles his sarcasms. He will certainly not accomplish lightly an action that requires mature deliberation. Besides, the height of the sun counsels the siesta.

Followed by all the children of the octopus, Mao draws away superbly.

Any initiative is assumed to be beneficial by the instinct of imitation and solidarity. Moreover, so many events and so much intellectual effort have numbed brains. Mao's possibly-reckless words and advice are supported by the certain desire of entrails and universal lassitude. In small groups hand in hand, the indigenes gradually cheer up and quit the bluff. They carry on their shoulders the still-inanimate body of the wise old man, whose limbs hang down to the right and the left.

The immolated gods remain lying there, alone.

But not for long.

The pointed muzzle of Ratari, the burrowing mouse, appears at the entrance to his hole. He takes two steps, pricks up his ears, looks the recumbent forms up and down with his round eyes, and advances in two or three hops. A few minutes later, the entire tribe is at table, fangs in play, disputing the lacerated flesh with shrill whistles.

They do not have it to themselves for long.

Black dots surge forth from all the corners of the sky. They draw nearer, increasing in size, and describe ever-decreasing circles. All kinds of raptors come in the response to the appeal of the cadavers, those from the sea and those from the aeries lodges in the high hills. With a great clatter of wings, enormous albatrosses, voracious seagulls, vultures and eagles descend upon the bluff; they sink their claws into the bodies, tearing bloody strips away with their hooked beaks. Before their assault, Ratari, frightened, is obliged to decamp, his belly half-full.

Already, however, the definitive cleaners are en route: those who are inescapable, who, in a matter of minutes, can make of whatever was still quivering with life a little while before, no matter how strong it was or how big it might be, into a small heap of bones, as white as pebbles.

In the vast subterranean cities of the red ants, between the roots of the great pandanus trees, the subtle call resounds:

Trara my sister,
Do you smell that odor?
Something out there's dead
Blood has been shed.
Form up, red ants
Move off, advance,
All come this way,
It's Trara's day!
It stinks, it lures
Trara endures!
March on, march on!
Trot hard, run, run!

In long, dense somber columns, Trara's people set forth. They scale the bodies, covering them, submerging them.

Under their mandibles, the flesh collapses and disintegrates. In vain, the birds of prey destroy thousands and thousands of the consumers with beaks and claws. The ants are still arriving, ever more numerous, ever more densely packed, climbing incessantly, rising like a tide. Their bites attack the raptors themselves. The latter renounce the struggle and fly away, with raucous cries of anger.

There is no longer anything on the promontory but a red seething mass. It quivers for several hours. Then, slowly, the ebb-tide draws the sated flood of cleaners back to their lairs.

All day long, Kouang has been ruminating his vengeance. The children have tried in vain to distract him. He has remained indifferent to their caresses and their games. In vain, Mémé has offered him ripe bananas. He is not hungry. In vain she has mixed guava juice and mango juice with coconut milk in a calabash. He is not thirsty. The savor of the murder is sufficient for him.

Toward dusk, however, a sudden hunger grips him. Yes, he has killed, but Koua is still dead. The itch to avenge her further torments him again. Who can tell whether a breath of life remains in the murderer? What if Kouang could kill him again, feel the vertebrae in his neck crack?

By the last rays of twilight, with a groan of desire, Kouang plunges through the foliage, the frightened inhabitants of which scatter, screeching. Pursued by the indignant objurgations of parrots woken from their initial sleep, he emerges from the woods and climbs the bluff again.

At the foot of the sacred mast there are five small heaps of white bones. They no longer have human form. The disconcerted Kouang sniffs them in vain. They no longer have any odor. Where Trara has passed, the work is done well.

Rara and Mémé pick up the polished skulls and stripped tibias curiously, amused by their shapes, and when they have examined them sufficiently they indulge themselves in a jesting simulation of combat. In their brown hands, femurs clash with a noise like castanets, and the festivities end with a general bombardment in which, transformed into inoffensive projectiles, the last debris of the skeletons is scattered.

Pensive and silent, Kouang contemplates them. And his obscure soul bleeds, with what a human would call incurable grief, the desiccating joy of vengeance, a yearning for oblivion and a desperate rebellion against pitiless Nature, who has endowed him with consciousness in order that his miserable rag can be simultaneously tortured by all the regrets of the past, all the horrors of the present and the desolate vision of the future.

IV

A few cables from the verdant isle, of which the gusts of the warm breeze sometimes bring the sweet scents, the light cruiser *Citoyen* is bobbing lazily at anchor. Everyone is on deck. Telescopes are searching the shore. The large launch is being lowered into the sea.

"You're intending to carry out a reconnaissance, then, Commandant?"

Commandant Kerfaouët turns the finely-chiseled clean-shaven face of a modern-sea-wolf toward the parliamentarian.

"Monsieur le député," he says, "as I've just had the honor of explaining to you, this region is one of the most inhospitable in the Pacific. Had it not been for the impudence of that Boche fish and the duty that requires everyone to attack the enemy, I would have avoided it like the plague, having the responsibility of your person, not to mention"—he turns to the young woman in question—"that of Madame de Vesnage and Captain de Pionne. Your anticlericalism will excuse me from affirming that it has required a special blessing from Providence, or a singular whim of the Devil, to get us through two thirds of the Murray Bank in a cyclone without leaving our carcasses there. While proceeding with indispensable repairs here, I'm going to see whether the currents might not have cast some trace of our blessed pirate ashore there.

"I imagine that it will be to more disagreeable to you than to me to make it known to the government that the little wooden craft that has the honor of taking you back to France has also had the honor of sending to the bottom the malefactor that was wreaking havoc in this region."

Monsieur le député Bedeau-Conflans inclines his chin with the reflective authority conferred upon him by his legislative mandate, his title of Vice-President of the Radical-Democratic Party and his functions as extraordinary delegate of the government of the Republic to the Far East.

Not having been included in the last ministerial re-shuffle, it has seemed to the new cabinet that there is occasion both to forestall the parliamentary effects of his disappointment and to utilize his civil value by confiding to him one of those propaganda missions that, at a cost of only a few tens of thousands of francs, have the double advantage of making the corridors of the Palais-Bourbon a little healthier and comforting our exotic compatriots in immeasurable proportions.

Accompanied by his secretary, Monsieur Pittagol, a diplomatic interpreter and graduate of the School of Far Eastern Languages, Monsieur le député Bedeau-Conflans has therefore been charged with bringing to our functionaries, our colonists and our indigenous protégés in Indio-China and Oceania the salutations of the motherland, and also studying means of intensifying the production in those regions of cotton, rice and patriotism.

Welcomed everywhere by the enthusiasm of the populations, the honorable delegate has had the old cruiser *Citoyen* put at his disposal for his return to France. His gallantry has admitted as passengers the young widow of the unfortunate Paul Sajol, whose defects, redeemed by an honorable end, ought not to cause it to be forgotten that he belonged to one of the best families in the Republic. He has also welcomed aboard Captain de Pionne of the Colonial Infantry, returning to the front.

Monsieur Bedeau-Conflans is devoting his leisure time to dictating a report to Monsieur Pittagol, which, delivered from the podium, will rally—with the exception of half the coalition—the applause of the entire Parliament.

The encounter with and probable destruction of the pirates will be a precious supplement to complete the justification of the député for having preferred the listening-post of the Palais-Bourbon and the moral revitalization of the Fatherland to his glory-free and peril-free ambassadorial duties.

Detaching his eyes from his binoculars, he continues his interrogation. "So this is the first time you've visited this region?"

"The first time. It is, moreover, quite possible that it has not seen our flag since the epoch when Dumont-d'Urville took possession of it in the name of France."

Exquisitely pretty, so pale and frail beneath her mourning-veil, Madame de Vesnage asks in her turn: "Oh, Commandant! Are we going to see savages? True savages? That would be delightful!"

Monsieur de Kerfaouët sketches an imprecise gesture. "It's doubtful. Nothing thus far reveals their presence. If they exist, however, prepare yourself for a few disappointments, for they belong to the lowest level— above the Boche, of course—of our wretched species. Isn't that so, Doctor?"

Doctor Boujade fashions the thick lips beneath his potato of a nose into a snout. He has dragged his carcass around all the seven seas. Beneath his gray hair, which is still thick, and behind the ludicrously-modeled barrier of his brow, his bilobate brain lodges an ample and composite arsenal of science and paradox, anarchic skepticism and humanitarian enthusiasm. Beneath his bushy eyebrows, still black, he darts the sharp gaze of his green eyes at the young woman—poor child!—and his southern accent rings out:

"It's certain that this region nourishes the most primitive races of Polynesia. If there are humans living on that reef, we'll have an unexpected opportunity to verify Jean-Jacques' theories regarding the noble savage. But is it still inhabited? However lightly the white man has touched it, he has had time to add his defects to those that were already undermining the indigenes..."

With a child-like impulse, Madame de Vesnage puts her hands together in prayer. "Don't tell me that they no longer exist!"

"I shall prolong them or resuscitate them to please you. All things considered, it's not entirely impossible that we'll unearth a few poor—very poor—relatives of Rarahu here."[15]

"What joy! And thanks to Monsieur Pittagol, perhaps we'll able to converse together!"

Monsieur Pittagol, bows hastily and deeply. The amity of Monsieur Bedeau-Conflans, of whom his father is one of the principal supporters, and his diplomas for the School of Far-Eastern Studies, have saved him the trouble of a long, monotonous and unhealthy sojourn in the trenches. It has been incumbent on him for three months, once the last strains of the *Marseillaise* have faded away, to translate for the edification of yellow or brown apes the speeches in which Monsieur le député

---

[15] Rarahu is the Tahitian heroine of *Le Mariage de Loti* (1880), a quasi-autobiographical novel by "Pierre Loti" (Julien Viaud), which made the author famous.

glorifies maternal France and stigmatizes the Boches' crimes against human rights. There is no doubt, given the applause that welcomes those speeches, either of the perfection of his linguistic skills or of the loyalty of those we administrate.

To that suffrage, however, flattering as it is, how infinitely preferable Monsieur Pittagol, a long-haired and sensitive poet, would find that of the exquisite creature whose fugitive apparition in Saigon has sufficed to fascinate him, whom he has been so excited to find aboard—and whose cry of joy so cruelly ripped his ears when, on seeing Captain de Pionne emerge on to the deck, she held out her arms to him and exclaimed: "You, Hugues! It's not a dream!"

When the universal cataclysm was unleashed, Laurette de Vesnage yearned, like all French women, to assume her share of the sacrifice. Beneath a white headdress, her excessively slender silhouette leaned over the beds of our wounded in a cosmopolitan caravanserai converted into a hospital. A few weeks later, it was her who, nailed to her bed, exhausted and feverish, was collecting the paternal grumbles of the old doctor. "You see, my dear child, I warned you that it was madness."

After three months, she was deemed to have recovered, at least partly. "Sun, chaise-longue and food." On condition of living like a mollusk, Laurette de Vesnage might continue to survive, idle and solitary, in the worldwide Gehenna.

One dark morning, in the grayness that enveloped her, the news arrived that Paul Sajol, the wretch whose name she no longer bears but who had never ceased to be her legal husband, had attempted, like so many others, to clean away the ordure of life by means of a beautiful death. He had joined the Colonial Infantry. The first privations had reckoned with his carcass, worn out by too many excesses. He was dying in a hospital in Saigon, of one of those maladies that have no mercy but can take any months to liquidate a man. From the hole into which what remained of his soul had withdrawn, an obsession had flowed without respite from his cracked lips and put a fire in his cheeks: "I should like to see Laurette; I should like Laurette to forgive me."

Thus, Laurette would be able to soothe the supreme anguish of a wretch who was a soldier of France, and her husband. In a matter of minutes, the decision was made.

Who or what can stop her? She is alone and useless. The train carries her to Paris. To her stubborn grace everything yields, including the most retrenched bureaucracies and the most formal orders.

Two months after receiving the dispatch, she crosses the threshold of the military hospital in Saigon with a firm tread. A specter lifts himself up on his meager bed, his eyes widening: "Laurette…it's you!"

Playing fair for once, death permits Paul Sajol to take another fortnight to die, without suffering, with brief intervals of lucidity, clutching the moist hand of his wife. When the wretch is laid in the ground, Laurette has no option but to leave. There is no time to lose if her remains are not to be swallowed up by the European cemetery beside those of her husband. The tropical climate has sharpened the malady undermining her. Fever takes hold of her every evening. A circle of iron squeezes her temples. Gratefully, she accepts the hospitality that the departing Monsieur Bedeau-Conflans offers her aboard his cruiser.

Yes, undoubtedly, there is a refinement of bitterness in going back, in descending into the inevitable without having received the adieu of the only being with whom a true bond still links her to the earth, and from whom nothing any longer separates her. Is it certain that the phantom of Hugues de Pionne, a soldier at Tonkin, had nothing to do with Laurette's departure for Saigon? Is it certain that, even beside the death-bed, his image was not floating between the cheeks of the dying man and the lips that murmured forgiveness to him? No matter! Laurette will go away without having seen him again. After all, it's for the best. A fugitive mirage would not have distracted the officer from his duty for an instant. He would have had the pain of seeing her again only to lose her again. It's for the best. She will go back without him even knowing that she has come...

She will go back with him.

From the depths of his jungle, Captain de Pionne has come to Saigon render an account of his ongoing operation against the pirates. There he has found the order to embark for the French front solicited many months before. A few hours suffices for him to liquidate everything. The hazard of a dinner has brought him face to face with the omnipotent delegate, who invites him to depart with him without waiting for the next liner...

"Only too happy, Captain, to assist a soldier to reach the post of honor to which the fatherland is calling him. You will be in gracious company..."

With amazement, Hugues de Pionne has learned that Laurette, to whom he intends to send a word of condolence in France, will be returning there with him, as a widow. It has required all of his soldier's stern will to suppress the surge that, when he saw her again, would have thrown his arms around the thin waist reaching toward him.

The excessively poignant seizure of the first moment has been succeeded by delightful days.

Yesterday, in the jungle full of fever, wild beasts and yellow bandits, death was staring the officer in the face. He will confront it again tomorrow, lurking in the forests of Argonne, on the cliffs of Champagne or in the Flanders mud. Between the two mortal death's-heads, God alone knows how, the miracle of his sunlit adolescence has been resuscitated: Laurette de Vesnage is beside him, free—and she loves him.

Yesterday, crushed by the universal nightmare, Laurette, at the bedside of a dying man, was chewing over all the bitterness of her spoiled life. Tomorrow, the enemy within will grip her once again—what doctor can cheat it?—with its murderous claw. Today, there is no more that this: over the golden and azure waves of the tropical sea, in the enchantment of indescribable sunlight and beneath the gleam of the Southern Cross, amid the soaring of albatrosses and the leaping of flying fish, in the midst of the Cytherean paradises that the corals have built and where Loti loved Rarahu, a ship of dreams is transporting her. She is free, she is in love. Beside her, Hugues de Pionne, the man she has always loved, is free and in love with her, as he has always been in love with her.

Everyone knows what there is in oneself and in the other. Everyone discerns death hanging over the other and oneself. But did the dungeons of the Terror prevent the lovers who met there from savoring supreme and indescribable voluptuousness?

Aboard the light cruiser *Citoyen*, which is bringing Monsieur le délégué Bedeau-Conflans back to France, a perfect and stoical idyll of amour has found its coronation.

There are fragile plants whose destiny is to put forth single, brief and splendid flower, and then die.

While the Captain, the député and the officers surrounding them continue to exchange their observations, Hugues and Laurette, leaning on the side of the vessel, avidly contemplate the cradle of coral and verdure huddled before them in the silk of the calm waters, streaked by great somber fish.

In a low voice, Laurette says: "Hugues, are you quite sure that we're here—that if I close my eyes and reopen them, all this won't have melted away? Can you imagine, Hugues, that in a little while—the captain has promised it—we'll be treading the virgin soil of the magical island we discovered as children, where we sheltered under coconut palms and banana-trees, whose fruits fascinated us when..."

The young woman's eyes go to the blue design ornamenting the officer's wrist, and the dark jade amulet that has never quit her own, even at the beside of the dying man. Then she goes on: "When we played at going to join the Uncle of the Crabs in the unknown retreat where he was surely waiting for us, on the other side of the world..."

They fall silent. An identical languor cradles them. Oh, to be able not to wake up from the dream that is connecting their decline to the first emotions of their puerile imaginations!

Exclamations run through the group. The Commandant turns to his passengers.

"The requested savages, Madame."

"Or rather," Doctor Boujade corrects, "the little savages; for, not to displease you, it's a couple of savage children—one of each sex—who are arriving in a coconut."

A pirogue has just emerged from the extremity of the bluff that delimits the bay in which the *Citoyen* has moored to the north. With a sudden flutter of the heart, Madame de Vesnage makes out two bronze puppets, who are making the spray fly with the rhythm of their paddles...

In the nascent dawn, on emerging from Kouang's grotto, Raramémé have perceived, facing them, in the midst of the waves, the surprising whale-mountain that has sprung from the bosom of the sea. Before that prodigy, more sedate minds would conceive a great dread and think, before anything else, of warding off the peril that it conceals, but Raramémé have the same curiosity that drives scatterbrained birds into the mouth of a rattlesnake and young monkeys to stick their fingers into the depths of shells to seize the secret creature murmuring within. With a single impulse, they bound toward the light bark pirogue, push it into the water and put to sea with all the vigor of their little muscular arms.

All the same, as they draw closer, they experience a little fear. The monster is bristling with a chaos of horns, darts, mouths and teeth. A terrible respiration emerges from its breast and pale figures, human in appearance, are moving on its back.

Mémé formulates the discovery and the apprehension. "I can see white gods. Perhaps they're evil!"

Perhaps. But Rara knows many prayers. Then too, he is very strong. Furthermore, his eyebrows are raised. On the largest tree on the island—for it is an island of sorts—an excellent sign appears. Colored red, white and blue, the same totem flourishes there that flutters over the mast, at the foot of which the stinking gods were massacred for having wanted to cast it down.

Authoritatively, Rara affirms: "These white gods are good. And do you see, Mémé, they're calling us..."

Toward the hands that are making amicable signs to them, Raramémé, who release their paddles, raise their cupped gilded palms. A rope-ladder is hanging down the cruiser's side. Rara swarms up it like a cat. Mémé climbs up after him.

They emerge on to the gangway and stand there, intimidated, their hearts beating, mute and motionless, before the semicircle that surrounds them...

"Monsieur Pittagol," says the Commandant, "if Monsieur le député will permit, I shall appeal to your talents. Deign to explain to these young chimpanzees that we have come with the most benevolent intentions, and that there is sugar and necklaces for them if they will kindly answer our questions."

By turns, Monsieur Pittagol addresses Raramémé in Chinese, Malay and Kanak.

They listen to the unthreatening music with an indecisive smile. Avidly, their nostrils flared and their ears pricked, their keen eyes search the faces, the garments and the strange décor deployed before them. More than apes, their slender figures do not displease Monsieur de Kerfaouët, reminiscent of a couple of gazelles or fearful roe deer, which a single clumsy gesture might put to flight.

"They're delightful," sighs Madame de Vesnage.

"Not very chatty, unfortunately," mutters the Doctor, "although Monsieur Pittagol is jabbering away so mightily..."

Suddenly, though, the young woman, unable to retain a scream, takes a step back. Rara's keen eyes are fixed on her hand. He has made a strange whistling sound and bounded toward her like a little panther. His agile brown fingers have seized the jade amulet and are fondling it. He is staring unintelligible syllables, devouring it with his eyes.

Captain de Pionne makes a movement to pull him away gently. Suddenly, Mémé is clinging to his wrist. She places her forehead on the tattoo that ornaments it. Then, with the same gesture, the two children point to the blue designs on their breasts, which reproduce the fetishistic animal with minute exactitude, and from their lips emerges a wild and bizarrely lilting chant:

> Click, clock,
> Mock, knock
> I have pincers and armor-plate.
> Click, clock
> Crock, block
> From Rahuo comes my race, my fate.
> Click, clock,
> Block, mock
> Blood will survive!
> Kroum is alive!

With an indescribable amazement and an intimate excitement, Laurette feels the radiant face of the brown boy stroking her fingers. Mémé is purring over the captain's wrist. They only pause to uncover their white teeth in youthful bursts of laughter, and to resume the refrain more loudly:

> Blood will survive!
> Kroum is alive!

On the golden strand framed by black coral reefs, the entire tribe of the Oyas has assembled. They are gravely contemplating the immense whale-mountain that rose above the water last night, and whose redoubtable breath, competing with that of Hakarou, is rising into the calm air in dark spirals.

There is no hesitation over its nature. In mythological epochs, the traces of whose memory is conserved by the elders, similar monsters have made fleeting appearances. They have issued from the soft Entity that surrounds the ocean in all directions. In their flanks and under the singular trees that protrude from them, white gods are lodged, whose magic is terrifying.

At any time, such an arrival would excite legitimate apprehensions. They are more acute by virtue of recent events. It is very dubious whether the Oyas have behaved exactly as they should with regard to the pale and fetid gods who disembarked on the island the other day.

When old man Manga-Yaponi emerged from the coma into which the irritable god with the lunar cranium had plunged him with a punch, he was able to take account of the sequence of events. He has heard the story, and had its details repeated several times over. His lips have not articulated any judgment, for Manga-Taponi does not waste futile words.

At the evening assemblies, however, everyone has observed the severity of his face. Undoubtedly the facts have awakened contradictory spirits in him. Who could be astonished by that? Surely, sins have been committed. They will be dearly expiated, for divine rancor is implacable.

Thus, the appearance of the whale-mountain has excited alarm. All evidence suggests that its coming is linked to the defective welcome that the Oyas gave to the gods that preceded it. It is pregnant with punishments and reprisals. In the anguish of what it conceals, the women dissolve into lamentations and cover their heads with sand, but the faces of the men remain serene. What must be, will be.

Manga-Yaponi knows the right thing to do. On his orders, the members of the tribe have donned their most beautiful necklaces and their most decorative loincloths. Their hair is laden with flowers and crowns. Collections of guavas, oranges, yams and coconuts have been assembled. Crouching on the ground, more intrigued than terrified—what madmen would remain concentrated on anguish for the future?—the indigenes contemplate the monster from which a motor-launch has just drawn away.

Thirty men have taken their places on board. They are armed to the teeth with rifles, sabers, pikes, grenades and machine-guns. The captain has entrusted command of the vessel to Lieutenant Le Guédec. Accompanying them are Dr. Boujade and the interpreter Monsieur Pittagol, because of their knowledge of mores and languages. The strange predilection manifested by the two savage children for Madame de Vesnage and the Captain has decided Monsieur de Kerfaouët, not without having his ears bent, to add them to the expedition.

There is a well-founded presumption that the welcome will be peaceful. Nevertheless, all precautions have been taken and precise orders given. Monsieur Le Guédec will limit himself to a brief reconnaissance, remaining in close communication with the cruiser which will open fire at the first signal. In the case that the attitude of the population remains entirely satisfactory, the Commandant and Monsieur Bedeau-Conflans will come ashore in their turn.

Hugues and Laurette are sitting side by side. Curled up at their feet, the bronze children are twittering, smiling at them. At the idea that a danger might threaten the woman he loves the officer is frowning, and his eyes are searching nervously, but Laurette has abandoned herself entirely to the mad charm of the adventure. It would be no more prodigious to be living "Little Red Riding-Hood" or "Puss-in-Boots."

On the beach, the coppery silhouettes are moving back and forth; it is impossible to detect the slightest sign of hostility. It is nevertheless preferable not to be hasty. Monsieur Le Guédec searches for a landing-place and the motor eases down. Faces can be made out now, hair ornamented with flowers, waving arms and imploring palms. A perfumed exhalation rises from the land, like a kiss.

Laurette stammers, ecstatically: "Hugues! Hugues! It's too delightful! Look at that old man..."

Standing on the planking, Raramémé show themselves to the surprised eyes of the tribe, and Rara's piercing voice shouts: "Here are the children of the crab. With them are the white gods of the crab. Our blood is the same. The crab is powerful. Honor to the ancestor."

At the unintelligible statements, Monsieur Le Guédec has tightened his lips. Beware of treason!

The machine-gunners are on the alert—but a rumor that seems joyful runs through the population. All heads bow down and strike the ground.

"One might think that they were stuck," opines the quartermaster, Lancosme, who is a child of Pantruche.[16]

How Raramémé comes to be in the company of the white gods is too complicated a matter to be clarified, but their presence is a good omen. The boy's finger points out a profound inlet in the reefs to the lieutenant,

---

[16] i.e. a Parisian, Paris having been given the nickname Pantin [puppet], corrupted by argot into Pantruche.

which can even accommodate a giant pirogue. With measured beats of the propeller, the launch moved forward again. A dozen indigenes run forwards, waving palm leaves.

"Land," commands Monsieur Le Guédec. And immediately: "Pay attention, lads! It's time to keep your eyes open!"

He leaps out first, followed by Monsieur de Pionne and the capering Mémé. Two sailors are behind them, revolvers in hand.

Rara guides Laurette by the hand

"She's not hard on the eyes, the chick!"

The little group reaches the beach in a few strides, and while Lancosme remarks on board: "Good landing. Let's make favorable contact," Manga-Yaponi advances to meet the gods.

He raises his trembling hands above his head. With one voice, at his signal, the entire tribe manifests the spirit of submission that is within it:

Honor to the gods so white!
Honor to the gods of might!

When the last ululations of the chorus have died away, the sage pronounces the speech suggested to him by his experience in a guttural voice.

"Unknown gods, who come from the great soft Entity, the valiant people of the Oyas salute you. We know that you are strong and that we are weak. Command, therefore, and we shall obey. We are not unaware that anger is boiling within you: the breath of the monster spitting out there, and the rumbles of the smaller one from its belly, from which you have emerged, have warned us. We do not know exactly why, for our intelligence is limited, but we suppose that it must be connected with the story of the gods with the penetrating fumet who preceded you and whom we have perhaps not treated exactly according to their merits. That occurred because the sublime fist of one of them struck my face so violently that my spirit, in which the wisdom of the people resides, was expelled therefrom for several hours—and I fear that during that time, deplorable errors might have been committed. We are all ready to expiate them, as is just, by the sacrifices that you indicate to us. Since two among you are united by the sign of the crab with these precious children, we hope that you will not be too demanding. In any case, try to express yourselves clearly, for we are very frightened and our weakness has difficulty understanding the language of the gods."

Having spoken, Manga-Yaponi, the sage, immediately prostrated himself. The tribe resumed their chorus.

Honor to the gods so white!
Honor to the gods of might!

Monsieur Le Guédec consults Monsieur Pittagol. "Monsieur," he says, "are you able to translate that speech for us?"

With perfect honesty, Monsieur Pittagol is obliged to admit that the detail is not clear to him. The indigenes' language is evidently a Kanak dialect, but it is corrupted or very primitive, and the tonic accent bizarrely modulated. He will need some practice to grasp its finer points. The essential thing is that these worthy people are full of good will and desire to testify it to their guests.

Monsieur Le Guédec nods his head. Without the aid of Monsieur Pittagol, a graduate of the School of Far-

Eastern Languages, he would have known exactly as much.

"Do you think you can explain to them that France is very powerful, that she does not wish them any harm—entirely to the contrary—and that we are searching for a Boche submarine of which they might be kind enough to give us news. I leave it to you to decide how to bring the communication within the scope of their understanding.

Monsieur Pittagol pulls a face. "You will not be surprised, Captain, that it will be rather difficult to convey its substance to these primitive intelligences."

In a clucking voice, whose pitch rises as he speaks, he informs the Oyas of the love of the metropolis and the good offices that it expects of their loyalty. Gestures underline the vehemence of his words.

The Oyas listen deferentially to the god's chant and contemplate his dance respectfully. The harmony therein is beautiful, and occasionally, its sounds resemble human language, in a rather unexpected fashion. Naturally, though, the ensemble is incomprehensible. It is probable that the god is threatening the Oyas with atrocious tortures if they do not carry out his will. It is important above all not to irritate him, and for that, the best thing to do is to nourish him.

The old chief summons the women. They approach, fearful and curious, offering the visitors the fruits of which their hands are full.

"I see, Monsieur Interpreter, that you've begun by ordering us lunch."

Monsieur Pittagol smiles agreeably. "You're not unaware, Captain, that any entry into a relationship begins with a preliminary gesture of hospitality."

Madame de Vesnage has sat down in the sand. On her knees, Rara and Mémé heap perfumed treasures. She sucks an orange and nibbles guavas with her beautiful teeth.

"A thousand thanks, Monsieur Pittagol; all this is delicious."

While she pecks away, Rara and Mémé introduce the goddess, indicating to the homage of all the image of Kroum that hangs on her arm. Men and women approach, gathering around and touching the fetish tentatively. From the coiffure of a female who sketches the magic sign on her forehead the young woman detaches a tiara and puts it in her own hair. A murmur of pleasure and joyful hand-clapping welcomes that grace.

Monsieur Le Guédec, increasingly satisfied, opines cheerfully: "In truth, Madame, I believe that your magic is even more efficacious in winning hearts than Monsieur Pittagol's eloquence."

Captain de Pionne is the object of the most flattering demonstrations on the part of a few rustic beauties. Their noses linger complacently on his wrist. Laurette laughs as she has not laughed for fifteen years.

"Look out, Hugues!"

Lancosme observes from the corner of his eye. "He's on a lucky streak, the officer. Not so disgusting, the girlies!"

The sailors' actions become bolder. The female savages are not restive, and their husbands feel honored by the familiarity of the gods.

Meanwhile, Monsieur Pittagol, vexed by a hint of mockery he perceives in Monsieur Le Guédec, has resumed his interrogations. He accompanies them with an increasingly vehement pantomime, furrowing his brows, pointing to the sea, striking the beach with his foot and imprinting footprints in the sand.

Monsieur Le Guédec, who is following him with his gaze, leans toward Dr. Boujade, and whispers: "I'm afraid..."

But he does not complete the sentence. An unexpected metallic clink is heard beneath the interpreter's boot. One his orders, the docile savages begin frantically clearing away the sand. In a few minutes, a long sheet metal pipe is revealed. Even if it were not possible to read on one end, in Gothic characters, *Wilhelmshafen*, the experienced eyes of the mariners would not be deceived by it.

Faces light up.

"My God!" cries Lancosme. "I do believe the Boche has ended up sinking."

The Oyas do not misinterpret the expressions of delight that the newcomers manifest. They are visibly pleased to have found one of the fetishes that the waters have expelled at the same time as the stinking gods. It is necessary to complete their pleasure. In a matter of minutes, various metal items are laid bare—among others, a piece of bulkhead on which the inscription *U-37A* is engraved.

There is no more doubt; the pirate has ended its career here. The recent tempest has pulverized it on the coral. But might some Boche have escaped? With a female savage on each arm, Patouillard, from Ménilmuche,[17] has drawn some distance away toward the edge of the coconut grove. He is seen to stop, looking down at the ground.

---

[17] The Parisian district of Ménilmontant, its name transformed by argot.

"Captain!" he shouts. "Come and have a look at this print and clap me in irons if it's local."

A circle forms around the footprint, Blurred as it is, it is not that of a bare foot. And there are others, even clearer: the nails of boots remain graven in the hard sand. There were survivors of the shipwreck. What has become of them?

On Monsieur Le Guédec's instruction, Manga-Yaponi is brought to the footprints. The officer shows them to him and squeezes his arm.

"Where are they?"

The old sage bows his head submissively. It is in order. Today's gods are demanding the others. Whatever might come of it, it is necessary to satisfy them. The old man points to the forest and, beyond it, the invisible bluff where the unfortunate carnage was accomplished at the foot of the sacred sign. Seizing Monsieur Le Guédec by the hand, he indicates to him that he is ready to guide him.

All that is much clearer than it would have been had Monsieur Pittagol served as an intermediary. The Boches are on land; the savages only want to get rid of them. Monsieur Le Guédec is burning with the desire to run after them forthwith, but the orders are formal; he telegraphs the ship.

Wreckage attests indisputable destruction of submarine U-37A. Some Boches seem to have escaped. Indigenes, whose excellent disposition I confirm, appear to be offering to deliver them to us in interior of island. Can I go?

Immediate response: *Wait for us.*

On the flank of the *Citoyen*, activity is discernible in the commandant's launch.

Laughing, Dr. Boujade says to Monsieur Le Guédec: "I'll wager that the Delegate General won't leave the responsibility of being the sole representative of France here to the Commandant."

A few minutes later, the launch lands. Ordered aboard, Monsieur Le Guédec offers an account of events. The attitude of the natives is entirely amicable. The Boches, if any have escaped, are certainly devoid of any means of resistance. With twenty men, Monsieur Le Guédec is ready, if the Commandant will authorize it, to go an collect them.

Monsieur Bedeau-Conflans intervenes, however. "Let me claim the honor, Commandant, in my capacity as delegate of the government of the Republic, of taking part in this operation."

"This vote-winning operation," Monsieur Boujade completes, in a whisper.

The Commandant represses a smile. Indeed, in the député's constituency, this adventure, appropriately presented...

Bah! The pirate's end has put the chief in a good mood. "We'll all go together!"

Preceded y a picket of marines, the Commandant and the Delegate General emerge on to the beach. At their approach, the indigenes multiply their genuflections and onomatopoeias of welcome.

Monsieur Le Guédec introduces them to the venerable Manga-Yaponi, who prorates himself. Then his extinct eyes go from one to another of his interlocutors. The metal shining on the Commandant's garment seems to indicate a high rank. But the député, who has put on his frock-coat, unbuttons it. He is wearing his sash. On his torso blaze the same colors that, up there, have been so carefully maintained on the totem-flag. Manga-

Yaponi touches his forehead with his fingers and places them piously on the relic.

A long murmur of admiration circulates among the savages, who flatten themselves on the ground, get up, and flatten themselves again. Faced with these testaments of loyalty, a pride that is simultaneously patriotic and personal fills the député. He proffers: "Does it not seem, Commandant, that these sympathetic populations have attained a degree of consciousness superior to the one you attributed to them? Before I express the sentiments of the government, Monsieur Pittagol, would you please tell them how touched we are by their respect for our national colors."

Meekly, Monsieur Pittagol pronounces a few syllables. Amicable clucking welcomes them. Everything is going well. No divine thunderbolts are falling. It is simply a matter of continuing to obey their clearly-formulated wishes.

In a matter of minutes, orders are given, and the little expeditionary column sets out.

Ratoupé and Prao were the first to clear the wreckage of the submarine. Their mime in the presence of the Boche footprints was the most expressive. They serve as guides for the advance platoon led by Monsieur Le Guédec. Behind them, protected by a double cordon of sailors, come the Commandant, the Delegate General, Dr. Boujade and Monsieur Pittagol, next to whom march Manga-Yaoni and half a dozen white-haired dignitaries. Rara leads Madame de Vesnage by the hand, and Mémé's hand is in the Captain's. On either side of the procession, for which the machine-gunners form a rearguard, the Oyas dance joyfully.

In a matter of seconds they have crossed the glossy barrier of the coconut palms and plunged into the underwood, amid the velvets and satins of grasses and foliage. The prodigious flowers are exhaling all their perfumes. The streaming waters are twittering. Here is a little black pond where frogs and terrapins are playing. A host of insects is buzzing. The deafening racket of the parrots is unleashed from one treetop to the next. A hail of coconuts, hurled by a band of monkeys, amuses the sailors greatly. Flying squirrels, extending their parachutes, launch themselves from one acacia to another. Two deformed beasts flee with enormous bounds.

"Kangaroos!" cries the young woman.

Lancosme observes, with satisfaction: "Nice! It's better than the Jardin des Plantes!"

Before this stunning vision, Madame de Vesnage becomes dizzy. Leaning on her cousin's arm, her light tread brushes the moss, scarcely cracking a twig. Raramémé flutter around her, offering her crimson, sapphire-blue and golden flowers, marvelous fruits, and a golden beetle. Inexpressively suave and calming forces swell her bosom. She stammers once again: "Are we not mad, Hugues?"

He replies: "Let's be mad, Laurette."

The bushes are more widely spaced. Gradually, the ranks mingle. At her side, the young woman finds Monsieur Pittagol. Today, her benevolence is universal. She smiles at him, and asks him, gaily: "Where are we, Monsieur Interpreter?"

Charmed, the young man shakes his head. "A long way away, Madame!"

"Not at all!" Dr. Boujade interjects. His southern accent is vibrant with emotion. "We're at home!"

Beyond the little bare heath, on the extremity of the bluff, the taboo sign now looms up. No matter how baroque and as bizarrely tattered the piece of cloth might be, and no matter how comical and imperfect the disposition of its colors has become, it is impossible not to recognize in that fluttering rag the simulacrum of the flag of the fatherland.

The député takes off his hat. All right hands are raised to the brims of képis or caps. Balissard opines in a low voice: "No matter what the old ones say, it does something to you, all the same."

They have arrived on the promontory, at the foot of the mast. Letters and numbers have evidently been engraved in the wood, but time has erased them. A few paces away there is a kind of stone cairn. Monsieur Boujade examines it, and utters an exclamation. They surround him. Scarcely hesitating, he deciphers the inscription, reading aloud.

"I take possession, in the name of France, of this island, which the Oyas who inhabit it call Oaleya. I have named the island Amélie and have raised the flag of the Nation here. Dumont-d'Urville, 14 October 1843."

Everyone falls silent. Heads are bared.

The Oyas perceive that the white gods are in communication with their ancestors. They crouch down and accompany their meditation with a muted chant:

This is the sign, the colored taboo
The gods have come from beyond the blue
May their will prevail and we be true!
This is the sign, the colored taboo.

The surprise cannot cause the principal objective of the reconnaissance to be forgotten.

"Nevertheless," grumbles Monsieur Le Guédec, "I see no Boches!"

"Excuse me, Captain; it wouldn't astonish me if I had one."

Advancing on command, Fusilier Garcin displays a skull that he has just picked up, in the upper jaws of which there is a glint of gold.

"Unless the people hereabouts practice dentistry..."

Other bones are found, buttons and fragments of uniforms. The Oyas easily understand what is required of them. In a few minutes, they collect all the funereal debris in a heap. Monsieur Boujade has no difficulty identifying five European skeletons. Just now there were five sets of prints in the sand. It really is here that the Boches ended their career.

How did the drama unfold?

It is futile to lie to the gods. They know everything, and only feign ignorance in order to set traps.

Meekly, Manga-Yaponi tells the story of the adventure. The elders of the tribe accompany his voice with an expressive mime. The fetid gods attempted to put their hands on the taboo sign whose colors are fixed to the abdomen of the god with the voice of thunder. Rightly or wrongly, they were massacred.

With an appropriately grave emotion, the député signals that he has understood. Perhaps a few details remain obscure, but there is no doubt of the striking proof of the fidelity devoted to tutelary France by this population of supposed savages.

Monsieur Bedeau-Conflans collects himself, adjusts his cravat and puffs himself up. "Commandant," he says, "I ask permission to address a few words to these worthy people, which Monsieur Pittagol will translate for them." As a nuance of skepticism might perhaps be passing over the officer's thin lips, the politician adds, emphatically: "In default of the detail of my allocution, they will

121

grasp the general meaning, and I would like to believe that it would not displease your brave mariners to hear the representative of the Republic pronounce French words on French soil."

Monsieur de Kerfaouët, who is in line for a promotion, is too polite, and attaches too high a value to the benevolence of the depute, to raise the slightest objection. In the midst of the respectful natives and the vaguely mocking "mariners" the pale god with the voice of thunder intones his chant:

"People of Oyas, Mariners of France…!"

In terrible modulations, with a pantomime that designates, by turns, the sacred mast, the skulls of the dead men, the sailors, the Oyas and his own breast, the Delegate General celebrates the loyalty of the tribe. Even in these distant regions, the luminous genius of France has made its imprint. It seemed to be almost effaced here, but it only required a sacrilegious threat to abolish it for the ineradicable fervor to reawaken in these primitive souls.

The pirate boat has come to grief on this faithful land. The survivors have paid with their lives for the impudent impulse that led them to attack the sign of liberty. France offers her thanks to her brothers the Oyas. She expected no less of them. She knows that their hearts, if not their lips, are similar to those of Frenchmen.

The depute raises his panama hat, turns toward the sailors and shouts: "Let us all unite, my friends, in the same cry: *Vive la République! Vive la France!*"

The mariners reply, in chorus: "*Vive la République! Vive la France!*"

And meekly, the Oyas stammer after them, clapping their hands: "*Biba Ulica! Biba Francea!*"

They are sincere. The god that thunders has the right. They accept his judgment. For their action, they will submit to the consequences that the voice rumbling within him demands.

That spontaneous ovation provides the delegate with a supreme exaltation. While Monsieur Pittagol translates his speech, he takes Dr. Boujade to one side. It is important that the memory of such a day should be materialized for the primitives. Monsieur Boujade detached from this breast the cross of the Légion d'honneur that is suspended there and hands it to him.

When Monsieur Pittagol falls silent, the god's thunder rises up again. His hand brandishes the blood-colored ribbon, and he bellows:

"Oyas, the government of the Republic ought to reward you for your behavior. Certain that my gesture will be ratified by the Minister of War, who is my good friend, I desire to attach the star of bravery personally to the breast of whoever among you distinguished himself most valiantly in the defense of the national flag."

He turns to his secretary. "I'm counting on you, Monsieur Pittagol, to explain to our friends the meaning of this symbol and the designation I expect of them."

A sweat of anguish beads the brow of the unfortunate man. "I fear, Monsieur le délé..."

Monsieur Bedeau-Conflans closes his mouth authoritatively. "Go on, Monsieur." And, speaking to Monsieur de Kerfaouët: "I don't doubt, Commandant, that you will approve..."

With tremulous lips, Monsieur Pittagol awkwardly ejaculates a few questions. Saddening as the discovery might be, he is beginning to suspect that he does not understand the language of the Oyas at all and that they do not understand a single word of what he says to them.

Proclaimed officially, however, that observation would be too humiliating to his self-respect and too prejudicial to his future for him not to struggle until the end.

He takes hold of the sign, waves it, places it on his breast and raises his index finger to mark that it is a matter of choosing a single recipient. Alas, distress strangles him. His hopes of being understood are, he imagines, slender...

He is wrong.

The Oyas have understood the imprecation of the thundering god, so ingeniously backed up by the little hairy clucking god, perfectly. The meaning of the crimson ribbon has not escaped them. In exchange for the bloodshed, the gods are asking for blood, but their clemency will be satisfied with a single victim: the one whose action unleashed the carnage...

From the old man's order, Rara cannot hide. Some distance away, on the spur of rock of which he is fond, near the place where he punished the murderer, Kouang is sitting pensively. His eyes are fixed on the immensity or distractedly turned away, for a few seconds, toward the unusual agitation of the humans...

In spite of his reluctance, when the child takes his hand, he allows himself to be led away. In front of him, the ranks of the Oyas part...

Monsieur Pittagol cannot believe his success. It is all working out. He stammers: "Monsieur le député, I believe that...the recipient..."

Monsieur Bedeau-Conflans deposits his hat on the grass, wipes his pince-nez, smoothes his hair. The elder Manga-Yaponi and the child of the crab advance toward him. Between them limps the postulant.

Monsieur le député raises an arm, and immediately lowers it again, disconcerted. Crazy laughter runs through the sailors. His Olympian smile darkens. Rudely, he asks his secretary: "What does this mean? You bring me...you bring me..."

If his exhaustion would permit it, Monsieur Pittagol would tear out his hair. He mumbles: "Be patient...a simple misunderstanding..."

"Which the simplicity of these people explains," Monsieur Boujade interjects. "The fist that crushed the cervical vertebrae I'm holding wasn't that of a man."

The député deigns to accept the explanation. "Pittagol, clear up this misunderstanding."

A misunderstanding that would make the bravest tremble, if anyone suspected the peril—for, at the sight of the white men, Kouang has felt his heart leap. His hair bristles. His nostrils dilate, sniffing. He grinds his teeth...but no, the odor is different. Besides which, the murder has left him with a kind of shame, a lassitude. He allows himself to be led away by the children, while Monsieur Pittagol resumes his calvary, gesticulating and speaking hoarsely.

Obscure as the will of the gods is, the subtle genius of Manga-Yaponi ends up glimpsing it. Undoubtedly, it is not exactly the death of the stinking ones that is blameworthy but the unworthy treatment inflicted on their remains. It was probably necessary to eat them or burn them. If Manga-Yaponi's spirit had not been wandering in limbo, he would never have tolerated that lack of respect, for which the inconsiderate initiative of Mao is solely responsible. Now that the Great Hairy One is not the appropriate victim, it is the author of such profanation that celestial vengeance demands.

Mao of the octopus, whose soul is cowardly, tries to defend himself as best he can. He is dragged pitilessly before the tricolor belly.

At this coup, no one can any longer be mistaken. The wrath of the god is satisfied. A redoubtable majesty illuminates his features. He draws the unfortunate to him, fixes the bloody mark to his phormium tunic, pronounces the anathema and embraces the condemned man grimly.

And the thunderous voice proclaims: "Let this ceremony, valiant Oyas, engrave this glorious day in your memory indefinitely. Let us once again cry, all together: *Vive la République! Vive la France!*"

With renewed delight, the Oyas slap their palms together, prostrate themselves and repeat, wholeheartedly: "*Biba Ulica! Biba Francea!*"

The celebration is concluded. The député grasps Monsieur Pittagol's shoulder in a familiar manner, as the latter recovers uneasily from his triumph, in order to signal his satisfaction; he will render an account of his services to the minister. In addition, Monsieur Pittagol will submit to him as soon as possible the text of a dispatch relating a summary of this glorious day.

"I shall ask you, Commandant, to transmit it by wireless to Papeiti, which will be instructed to cable it to Paris."

Followed by a company of savages, the detachment from the *Citoyen*, its mission accomplished, has quit the bluff and gone back into the forest in order to descend to the beach again. Rather tired, Madame de Vesnage is leaning more heavily on the Captain's arm. There is an ecstasy on his face.

"You know, Hugues, that we're going to stay here for a few days…"

Monsieur Bedeau-Conflans continues to perorate animatedly. He will employ his leisure in making a detailed study of the resources of the island and drafting a report. He has no doubt that transport, once organized...

He pauses momentarily, gazing in surprise and circumspection at a bizarre couple emerged from the river. Standing up on their backsides, Pippi-kuink and his companion salute Rara and Mémé by clapping their vestigial limbs, quacking gaily.

Monsieur Bedeau-Conflans leans over mechanically to grip his secretary's arm again. "We'll also send a telegram to my constituency..."

On the bluff, Mao has remained in a state of dejection, resigned to his destiny. Around him, the people of the octopus intone a brief mortuary hymn. Then the sledgehammer falls upon his head, extending him on the ground.

With trenchant flints and sharpened seashells, his flesh is divided up and put on skewers. The skewers are presented to the flames of a rapidly-erected pyre. And conscientiously, the people of his clan devour him avidly, in order that they might keep his spirit among them and that the accomplishment of the rites might finally appease the legitimate anger of the divine visitors...

On the beach, by the last gleams of the setting sun, the re-embarkation is taking place. Will the white gods disappear and dissolve again? Who can tell?

Rara and Mémé trot alongside their brethren of the crab. Is there not anguish in their velvet eyes when the latter separate themselves from their grip?

"How can we explain to them, Hugues, that we'll come back tomorrow?"

The young woman puts her arms around the boy, and then the girl, mingling her caresses with tender inflections, punctuated with kisses on the brown foreheads and coppery cheeks, which have an odor of small animals, the sea and all the perfumed plants of the marvelous forests.

The children accept the kisses, astonished, because the gesture is unknown to the Oyas. But when the boat draws away, and when the tribe, astonished by so many adventures, has dispersed, they draw closer to one another, join hands, and, hesitantly at first, alternately place their lips on one another's cheeks, and occasionally bring them together.

And they are infinitely pleased by the sweet discovery that they owe to the pale gods of the crab and the kiss.

V. THE FORTUNATE ISLE

Is the world about to sink into chaos again? Because of all the rage and love they have, humans are confronting one another, colliding with one another, massacring one another, on land, in the blazing atmosphere, and even in the depths of the sea. The entire effort of civilization is concluding in the most frightful catastrophe that has desolated the planet since the deluge.

Protected from the rest of the world by the girdle of reefs and gulf that surround it, Oaleya the fortunate is pursuing its peaceful, innocent and harmonious existence.

Patiently, the work of the coral raised it stone by stone above the abysses where the indecisive germs of being sleep. The great central fire sculpted its fragile architecture according to its whim. For thousands of years the wind brought dust, the rain rotted the stone, the sun vivified the mud, and the primitive homogeneity decomposed into an infinite pullulation of kingdoms and species.

To the top of the scale, but not very high, still in contact with the rest of animality, humankind has risen. Elsewhere, the megalomaniac vermin has broken the bridges behind it, claiming monarchy for itself, and the image of god, has suppressed and rejected its kin, has individualized itself excessively, has multiplied divisions, hierarchies and rivalries within its own bosom. The superior vertebra of the Oyas has not enlarged into the aristocratic and anarchic brain of a superbeast. They have not subjected the whim of Rahuo that has fashioned them to a drunkenness of pride.

They have conserved the obscure instinct of the links that subsist between the unities of species, and which subsist between the species themselves. They have an intuition of all the unknowns and all the ungraspables that surround them, and which undoubtedly have as much reality as themselves. Alongside the visible, they suspect the invisible. The undulating world of spirits does not appear to them to be more improbable than the one whose designs and colors they discern.

Besides which, everything that is today is merely the fugitive appearance of that which is eternally. On the great ocean of life, humanity is an oily patch in which the colors of the prism are reflected for a few seconds, and which, floating for an instant on the dormant waters, will dissolve there at the first eddy.

In the bosom of the harmonious creation, the Oyas unfurl their innocent, mechanical lives, little different from those of kangaroos, and not fundamentally different from those of corals. They are born, grow up, love, suffer, forget and die without making any great fuss about it. They are not obsessed with immoderate dreams. They accept their ignorance and their weakness. They do not revolt against the inevitable. They do think that they are any more eternal, or very much wiser or more sublime than a wisp of sea-spray, and do not imagine themselves to be kings or gods during the blink of an eye in which heaven has projected them from the wave that will break and swallow them up again.

Into drowsy Oaleya, protected by the immense swell of the Pacific and the laborious army of madrepores from the pernicious fever of the rest of the world, a gust of the universal cyclone has now precipitated a panting handful of the gnats with which it toys.

A wireless message has sent an instruction to Papeiti, which has transmitted a brief account of events to the Ministry of Marine.

Attacked by the Boche submarine *U-37A*, the *Citoyen* has been fortunate enough to sink it. The damage that it sustained during the combat, aggravated by a typhoon, has obliged it to lay up for a few summary repairs at Île Amélie.

A more detailed dispatch from the Delegate General has informed the President of the Council of the touching welcome given by the population to the envoy of the Republic.

It arrives in Paris at a time when the news is bad. Men are dying cruelly and with no result in Flanders, on the Somme and in the Woëvre. The Russians are buckling; defeatism is rearing its ugly head again, the ministry is shaky and the muzzled press is nervous. Let it be given exotic fodder. The edifying robinsonade is inserted between the news of the health of the kaiser (definitely attained by general paralysis) and the last communiqué from Champagne (we have captured two hundred meters of trench at Massiges), Mr. Wilson's latest note to Germany and the comforting impressions of a neutral regarding the famine in Berlin (people are eating bootlaces and brick bread there).

At the moment when inadmissible maneuvers are multiplying in which it is easy to recognize the hand of the enemy, and for which public vigilance is keeping its eyes open, news has reached us from the antipodes that ought to fill national confidence with a just pride. A dispatch from Papeiti has notified us that the cruiser Citoyen—*the democratic name of which tickles our ears agreeably—has succeeded, in circumstances that will be described precisely at a later date, in destroying the re-*

131

doubtable Boche submarine whose exploits have been terrifying Polynesia for three months.

Constrained, in order to make repairs, to put into Île Amélie—which has been French since Louis-Philippe, but which, situated far away from the major sea-lanes, has not received a visit from any ship of the metropolis since time immemorial—it has been given the most enthusiastic welcome by the indigenes. Delegate General and député Monsieur Bedeau-Conflans, in an eloquent speech admirably translated by the official interpreter Monsieur Pittagol, has expressed to that sympathetic population the gratitude of France, and has decorated one of its most eminent chiefs with his own hands.

We are glad to add that, in recognition of his outstanding services, the Minister of Marine has just awarded the croix de guerre, with palm, to Monsieur Bedeau-Conflans, whose resolute attitude has been worthy of our finest traditions. Public irony is sometimes lavished—almost always unjustly—on certain distinctions awarded to our parliamentarians, but there will be unanimous applause for a measure that simultaneously honors the patriot in question and a government capable of recognizing his services...

The wireless message informing the député of this distinction also invites the commandant of the *Citoyen* to proceed with his repairs without excessive haste. In any case, let him wait new orders that might perhaps prescribe a detour on the homeward journey.

To tell the truth, if the united socialists attempt a definite assault on the cabinet, it would be better if Monsieur le député Bedeau-Conflans were not yet reintegrated into the Palais-Bourbon. He is a potential ministerial candidate. The government would be much surer of his loyalty if it were impossible for to him to withdraw it. His proxy votes are admirably placed in the hands of the Undersecretary of State for Moral Replenishment.

Such is the combination of circumstances that, in the midst of cosmic horror, has becalmed Hugues and Laurette in the most magical oasis.

By the fault of destiny, and their own, they were leading a lamentable chaotic life. Shadows were oppressing them. There was no light on the horizon. Young as they are, death was already leaning over them; they could not drive it back...

With a flick of a magic wand, everything that was crushing them has melted way.

Here they are, in a Cytherean paradise, free, palpitating with love, cradled in the soothing splendor of an inviolate Nature.

It has not required more than forty-eight hours for the severity of orders to be relaxed. The pacific temperament of the Oyas is as manifest as the resources of the welcoming isle are varied. At the edge of the beach of disembarkation and the coconut palms, Monsieur de Kerfaouët has established a permanent station. A few luxurious tent-shelters have been appended to it. The two most comfortable are occupied, one by Madame de Vesnage, the other by the député and his secretary. A third is shared by Dr. Boujade and Captain de Pionne. Thus, the député and the doctor can devote themselves at their leisure to the labor of their research.

"And the lovers," the Commandant murmurs, "will be able to flirt at their ease."

To flirt?

Oh, that harsh and unconstrained Anglo-Saxon term is a poor translation of what unites the officer with the tormented features and his fragile companion. Nor is it what the imagination of the young ensigns on the ship, little inclined to refinement in the chart of tenderness, believe that "the soldier and the little widow are getting up to."

Although it would seem stupid to those gentlemen of the forecastle, the embraces of the puerile and chaste lovers are limited to the exchange a few glances charged with emotion and a few slow pressures of their trembling fingers.

They love one another. They love one another with all the unsatiated tenderness and need for love that is within them, but the rare, unique amour in which they commune is not that which knots feverish arms around necks and sticks lips deliriously together.

If Hugues begged or demanded, would Laurette refuse herself? No, since she is entirely his, but even if male temptation troubles him, a firm, gentle and implacable will represses it—because, thanks to him, she is no longer in pain; and because he might soon disappear himself, without remorse. What separates them—and what unites them—is the very quality of the sentiment that exists between them. If they cannot be lovers, it is because, for a very long time, with the best of themselves, they have loved one another in a finer fashion, too purely.

In the atmosphere of the marvelous isle, it is their twin childhood that flourishes again, dilates and blossoms. Under the somber crowns of the trees, beside the dark waters, in this great magnificent garden, to the accompaniment of the murmur of the ocean over the coral, everything that has bruised and aged them is abolished. In the bosom of equatorial Nature, their childhood tenderness is still the same, but multiplied tenfold in their adult hearts. There are no words to express what impregnates them. The only words that rise to their lips are the innocent words of old, those of the time when they played together in the old familial dwelling, when they trotted side by side on the shore of the same immense ocean.

Laurette's fingers play with a porcelain animal with a speckled back.

"Do you remember, Hugues, the glass case with the seashells, the marvelous stories that they whispered in your ear, and which you repeated to me in the evenings?"

With the tip of his cane, Hugues teases a sea-spider with a rough and spiny back.

"Do you remember Mitsou, Laurette—the wretched little alley-cat that we found half-dead in a ditch, and for which, fearful of abduction, we made a hiding-place, with the complicity of old Pauline in a corner of the broom-cupboard?"

They laugh as they have not laughed for years. Their wretched and poor existence has sunk into oblivion; even their adolescence has faded away. Nothing else survives but he magical mirages of the childhood epoch when the world's new dawn rose before their eyes…and now, they have the enchanted world in which their games took refuge to themselves.

A few heavy birds, whose tails drag along the ground, take flight in the clearing. Laurette claps her hands. "Oh! Hugues…birds of paradise! The *Nautilus* run aground in the Torres Strait[18]…do you remember?"

Rara and Mémé are their assiduous companions.

---

[18] In chapter 19 of Jules Verne's *Vingt milles lieues sous les mers* (tr. as *Twenty Thousand Leagues Under the Sea*).

Before the tent-shelters were installed on the shore, the children accompanied the officer and the young woman to the boat every evening and, sitting down, followed the launch that was taking them away with their eyes until it disappeared in the darkness. Every morning, at first light, they watched for their return, and swam out to meet the launch. Now that Madame de Vesnage spends her nights on land, the two children sleep at the entrance of her tent. They offer her their foreheads in the evening before she goes to bed, and in the morning, salute her awakening with twittering. They have soon learned a few words of French. Hugues and Laurette have grasped the fundamentals of the language of the Oyas, which are not very numerous. Thus they have become capable of conversing. Nevertheless, there are such abysses between them that the conversations in question cannot get far away from few very simple themes.

Well beyond that, however, above words, a subtle and penetrating intimacy has been woven between them.

And Rara and Mémé embody the empery of the fraternal isle. They incarnate the tender Nature that welcomes the young people, bandages them and coddles them. Perhaps, in them, they find vague echoes of themselves, such as they might have been, if the evolution of the centuries had been different. They too live a single life. They too are separated by a gulf from the rest of the world. That gulf, a mysterious impulse of the brown children has abolished between them, the first moment they met.

Laurette declares to Hugues, laughing: "I believe in the kinship of the crab, you know."

And Hugues replies, laughing in the same way: "Might I hazard a confession, then? Do you know that there's a family resemblance between Mémé and you?"

That familiarity is the object of jokes among the young officers of the *Citoyen*: "Admit that those lovers are funny people, needing to drag an escort of savage kids behind them..."

It is true. Hugues and Laurette feel more at peace when the children are there. In their intimate conversation, in spite of everything, there are lightning-flashes of the cruel past and the atrocious future, and starts of troubled anguish. When the children are playing around them, they are better protected against destiny and against themselves. If Laurette is better, Dr. Boujade is the first to congratulate the influence of the crab.

In the exceedingly handsome and exceedingly gentle white gods that have come to them, Raramémé have welcomed without astonishment—why be astonished when everything is mysterious?—those for whom they were waiting. The people of the crab maintain the divinity of Rahuo, who is the Great Crab. Once, they were numerous, and there was the Ancestor, but now their mark is almost effaced. While the people of the octopus, the people of the armadillo and the people of the kangaroo experience a comfort and an enrichment in holding one another by the hand, in living and eating together, Raramémé remained poor and alone. They have only had Kouang.

But the crab ought not to perish, nor should the blood of the Ancestor dry out. Those who had to come have come—and in them, Raramémé have not only found powerful friends, but what they need to raise them up by a degree in existence. You are the most miserable of the miserable if you live enclosed in yourself. Already, Rara lived in Mémé, Mémé lived in Rara; now they also live in Houga, who is Hugues, and above all in Lauritea, who is Laurette. Thus is formed a new organism, which is much more perfect. To the young woman, without Mémé being jealous, Rara has given his brown forehead, on which she so gladly places her lips. To Houga, Mémé has given her velvety cheeks, which he brushes every evening with a kiss. They are no longer two little savages, a socialite and a French officer, brought together by a whim of chance; they are that original creature, that close, rich and intimate association Raramémé-Hougalauritea

It is something like a fraternity of four, in which the little brethren have for the older ones the caress of a cat purring around its master, the unreserved adoration of a faithful dog toward its chosen one, whose gesture determines thought, morality, life and death.

The fortunate isle is full of beasts, flowers, stones and waters that are amicable. Nevertheless, Raramémé were unable escape the fear of invisible or furtive demons that crawl, float and glide, surrounding the living with traps and threats. Now they no longer fear them. United with the white gods, they form a permanent conjuration against which the worst spells will run aground. Fortified by Lauritea's matinal kiss, they can brave all the ambushes of the day. Enriched by her evening kiss, what revenants can trouble their dreams?

With their friendship, they have associated Kouang.

At first, the Hairy One kept his distance from the strangers, manifesting distrust toward them. His formidable stature, the rolling of his eyes and the grinding of his teeth did not fail to cause the sailors some anxiety. Perhaps, but for the Commandant's formal orders, given to the crew on Monsieur Boujade's insistence, he would have been shot.

"You tell me, old chap, whether the fellow has a limp...in the church back home, there's a Devil who resembles him like a foster-brother."

Thanks to the chief, Kouang has been respected. Joking has even succeeded malevolence; attempts have even been made to domesticate him by offering him biscuits, sugar or a glass of eau-de-vie, but Kouang, whom no threatening gesture seems to excite, has remained insensitive to all flattery. Lancosme has expressed his resentment at seeing his advances disdained to his comrades in picturesque terms: "What do you expect, lads? That ape only keeps company with toffs—you and me aren't distinguished enough."

Indeed, Hugues and Laurette are the only ones who have won the monster's familiarity. Perhaps, in the first days after Raramémé adopted them, he felt an obscure jealousy. Hugues has kept watch on watch him, his hand on his revolver, after seeing the giant's eyes light up with an ambiguous gleam while fixed on the young woman with the two children laying around her. The first impulse of fear having passed, however, Laurette has allowed the children to lead her to him and has placed her gentle hand on his rough shoulder.

Through the hairy pelt, the caress penetrated into the lair of the heart. Beneath the enormous bushy eyebrows, at the base of the embryonic brow, on the two sides of that which is not a muzzle, the two eyes contemplated the young woman strangely, with a sadness so penetrating that, seized by a sudden anguish, she was unable to help murmuring: "Oh, Hugues, can you believe that he's only an ape?"

So Laurette does not behave with Kouang as with a domestic animal, but rather as if he were a distant relative, poor, unhappy and simple-minded, speaking an unknown language, but to who one shows all the more respect because impenetrable sensitivities are contained within him, easy to offend. "Come on, Doctor, admit that he's much closer to us than a Boche."

Dr. Boujade often shares, along with Kouang and Raramémé, the two cousins' strolls in the flowery island. Oh, what a rage would shake the bones of Dr, Klagenmeyer, in the grave where they have been assembled, if he discovered that the prodigious anthropopithecus that he extracted from the equatorial forest has become a subject of observation for a foreign scientist! How his fury would increase if he were able to suspect that to the fantasist in question, a demi-crackpot, having no notion of the methods of German science, the unique phenomenon only suggests crazy revelations, worthy of H. G. Wells or Restif de la Bretonne.

If his sojourn in Oaleya is, indeed, filling Monsieur Boujade with an increasing passionate delight, it is not because he has found there a new opportunity to measure, massacre, dissect, vivisect, classify, govern and exploit. It is simply that the spectacle it offers is exciting in his elongated cranium his impenitent faculty of imagination, and causing the most bizarre hypotheses to take root there.

His Marseillais mannerisms, his despotic frowns and the trumpeting of his speech, as well as the few worlds of the Oya language he has assimilated—much more rapidly than Monsieur Pittagol—have rapidly revealed his magical abilities to the indigenes. He is able, by means of talismans that are unique to him, to chase away the deadliest spirits and to summon the most helpful. Without suction, by the simple application of piquant water and a bandage, he has cured an inflamed open wound in Tapo-Harus' thigh. A purgation had dispelled the hydras that were battling in the belly of Wang-toa. A potion has reduced Rongo-mai to silence, who was shaking Mairea's chest with a hacking cough. Titi-Hai had been making Moilea limp for a week; the new sorcerer has expelled him in a night. Touga had taken the spirit of Haï-Pou far from his head; the white sage has brought it back from the escarpments of the promontory where it was already wandering.

Thanks to his art, and thanks to the forbearance of the indigenes, who facilitate his investigations, Monsieur Boujade has entered into their intimacy in a matter of days.

A companion of the young folk in the fortunate isle, under the escort of the ape and the savage children, he never wearies of roaming the valleys, the hills, the meadows, the woods and the steep gorges, accumulating observations, framing ludicrous hypotheses...

Emerging from the coconut grove, he perceives Hugues and Laurette sitting on the sand. The young woman is mischievously teasing Pippi-kuink, his spouse and their twins; lying beside her, Raramémé are alternately crunching raw crayfish, which are exquisite, and caramels, which make them grimace at first. A short distance away, the monstrous Kouang is considering them pensively.

Monsieur Boujade takes his camera from its case and aims it at the group.

At the sound of his approach, the young woman raises her head; she threatens the intruder with her finger. "Well Doctor, aren't you going to apologize for the indiscretion?"

"I apologize, Madame, but I'll take advantage of it. A pretty social snapshot for the *Excelsior*."

The click of the shutter has fixed the scene. Intrigued, Rara approaches the fat man with a soft tread.

"It interests you, young clown? Look at the little beast.

The boy handles the apparatus, turns it over and over, sniffs it, searches it with his fingers, touches his forehead and returns the magic box to the god. It is another of the spells that are so abundant in the white men's hands. It does not smell good, nor is it pretty, or pleasant to eat. Better that Mémé does not touch it, in case something bad emerges from it.

The young woman indicates to the doctor a mountain of fruits and berries beside her. "Come and share the meal that I owe to my providers."

The fat man settles down jovially. "Who could refuse the opportunity to break bread—I mean, to suck mangoes and nibble guavas—in the company of a pretty lady, a hero of the Great War, a pithecanthropus and two young cannibals?"

Madame de Vesnage is busy rolling one of Pippi-kuink's offspring in the sand before the placid eyes of its parents. It wriggles furiously, hissing nasally with all its might, trying to bite. The indignation experienced by the young woman permits her victim to recover its aplomb and escape, clicking its beak.

"Two young cannibals! Doctor! Is it really our little companions that you mean? Don't forget that, via the crab, they're my distant cousins..."

"Madame," says the Doctor, gallantly, "from you, everything is precious to me, even a bite. As for your young relatives, I'd prefer to think that they prefer coconuts, but I'll confide to you in a whisper that the destiny of our recently-promoted legionnaire has been a troubling revelation to me. Monsieur Bedeau-Conflans testified his astonishment to me the other day that he had not seem him again, with his breast ornamented with the glorious insignia. Alas, certain calcined and freshly-gnawed bones that I picked up at the foot of our sentry-mast incline me strongly to believe that he terminated his career in the bellies of his compatriots.

"I wouldn't even be surprised if, by a logical process whose detail I can't work out, it was the very distinction of which he was the object that precipitated the treatment in question. Believe, furthermore, that it is indispensable in these latitudes to renounce any paltry prejudice you might perhaps be nursing with regard to anthropophagy. That custom has for its bases a legitimate horror of wastage, a sentiment of filial piety toward the remains of our ancestors and an appetite for perfection analogous to our scholarly hunger. It is by consumption that we assimilate most surely the wisdom and virtues of our peers. Having no books to devour here, one can at least devoir the distinguished personalities whose genius might have written them, and whose exploits might have filled their pages..."

Arresting the young woman's protests with a gesture, the Doctor concluded: "Moreover, I wouldn't be surprised if those respectable customs were in their decadence. Here, as elsewhere, pitiless progress is besmirching the most sacred traditions. It might be that in this region, the anthropophagic doctrine is as outmoded as that of *Action Française* in a Parisian brain of the 20th century.[19]

---

[19] *Action Française* was a far-right newspaper edited by Léon Daudet, a writer with whom Lichtenberger had probably been acquainted while Daudet was still at the heart of the Republican movement and Lichtenberger was active in the same cir-

Lazily extended amid the seaweed, the young woman is playing distractedly with the hair and necklaces of Mémé, lying alongside her. Her gaze is following the frolics of the parrots in the glistening foliage. She murmurs: "Where are we, Doctor? Isn't this the mot paradoxical place on the planet?"

"Perhaps, Madame. Unless it is only here that there is wisdom and truth, while the rest of the world is plagued by delirium. In sum, Madame, if universal history is exact, it does not seem that the excessive individualism into which Nature has finally lapsed has not produced such fine results that we have the right to treat other hypotheses with disdain. It's exciting, Madame, to discover here a sketch of what she was once able, momentarily, to dream.

"Evidently, from primitive protoplasm to present specialization, a path has been followed, but I've never been able to envisage without horror the sum of tortures and carnage at the price of which the distinction of species and the sovereignty of humankind has been effected. Oh, how revolting I always find the cruel imperialism of Noah, who refused to take in the Ark, doubtless because they ate too much, the sympathetic mammoths and other megatheria of the antediluvian era, and thus broke—the rascal—a few infinitely precious links in the great chain of being, which became so difficult to reconstitute!

"It's too late now to retrace our steps, alas—but Nature has amused herself by conserving here, as if in a secret casket, a sketch of what might have been. If the world had evolved like Oaleya, where an animal can be both mole and duck, or a rat and tortoise, where coral is

cles, before Daudet converted to reactionary opinions and Lichtenberger surrendered to disenchantment.

stone and flower, where an octopus is a star, where plants can be carnivorous and eat insects, we would not have seen unpleasant fissures hollowed out between species and individuals. The human species would not be so haughty in the titanic arrogance that makes it such an unsociable newcomer. More compassionate toward its poor relatives, it would at least have refrained from dissociating itself so much—and perhaps it would not be in the process of sinking into an atrocious regression.

"Oh, Madame, how sweet and how bitter it is for me to imagine that, if the system of Oaleya had prevailed, there would far more between you and me than the dream of fraternity that haunts our most impenitent humanitarians: the affinity that units the bees in a hive. You would be the rose and I the thorn on a single bush! But I fear that I might appear to you to be rambling. Forgive me, then, for leaving you to your young relatives and to our slightly-more-distant Hairy cousin. Inconvenient spirits are treacherously assailing Madame Nebitoua of the birds of paradise. In vain my colleagues Touritou and Patakuk are combating them with spitting, suction and other ingenious treatments. My sorcery is requisite to the rescue. I must go to the consultation..."

Slowly, hand in hand, Hugues and Laurette are walking along the beach. Kouang has moved away to search for the more substantial nourishments that are indispensable to him, which the thickets around the black pool contain. Only Raramémé are accompanying their friends. The tide is out. In the partly-uncovered submarine forests and palaces of coral, surprising fauna and flora of the waters remain captive.

"Let's go to the rock-pools, Hugues," Laurette proposes, "as we used to do."

They scale the rocky plateau, leaning curiously over the transparent pools in which mollusks scintillate, scaly rockets dart, or disquieting tresses undulate, from which heady saline odors rise up.

As swift as doradoes, Raramémé caper and gambol, holding out their hands, guiding their steps all the way to a rocky point swathed in seaweed. The young people allow themselves to collapse there, facing the sparkling splendor of the setting sun. Around them, the children continue to bustle. Mémé proudly deposits sea-urchins, starfish and sea-cucumbers at their feet. Harpoon in hand, Rara lies in wait for fish, strikes and hauls them out repeatedly, of every size and shape. A viscous and iridescent host soon accumulates, quivering, at the feet of the young officer and is companion.

The fishing over, Raramémé approach their friends. The boy places his finger on the amulet of the crab dangling from the young woman's wrist. He makes a long speech. Mémé repeats the final lines in a singsong voice. The whole rigmarole is utterly unintelligible. Nevertheless, Hugues and Laurette recognize one word therein, which designates the strange link that unites the savage children. With an understanding expression, both nod their heads in approval.

"Kroum, yes, Kroum."

Then Rara claps his hands—and heir pearly teeth shine between their lips. They are overjoyed that the white gods are deigning to participate in their fraternal ceremony. Crocking at their feet, in the serenity of the evening, they prelude the canticle of the race:

Tick, tock,
Knock, shock...

And now, from dark holes and deep pools, over the unctuous mosses and the black and hairy rocks, in all direction, pincers and feet surge forth, carapaces and round eyes, shiny and keen. The immense army of blue crabs comes running, concentrating, falling and fighting over the provender that is offered to them. Alarmed at first, seized by disgust, the young people watch the improbable feast with amazement. Raramémé sing, softly:

Click, clock,
Block, mock...

In a matter of minutes, the flesh is torn apart and swallowed. Then Raramémé clap their hands, intoning one last time the *leitmotiv*:

Let's take our pride
Away to hide;
Blood will revive,
Kroum is alive!

Around them, the blue crabs get up, brandishing their pincers, allowing them to fall back rhythmically, and then draw away, trotting sideways.

Bewildered, the young couple follow them with their eyes. It is a dream. Have they not always had it? Far away, very far away, on the Basque coast, at the foot of the cliffs of Ilbarritz, under the aegis of the distant uncle, have they not bound themselves in an infantile alliance with the deformed people whose image haunts his notebooks? A baroque sensation takes hold of them, as if, in spite of everything, this prodigious spectacle were not entirely new to them, as if it were awaking atavistic correspondences in them, at a vast distance...

147

Laurette grips her cousin's hand, digging her fingernails into it.

"Hugues, Hugues, doesn't it seem to you that once, already, somewhere...? Who are we?"

In low voices, Raramémé are conversing in an animated fashion—which is to say that each of them, alternately, is forming syllables that the other repeats, mutedly, as if to amplifying them. Something grave must be agitating between them.

From time to time they fall silent, seemingly looking within themselves, in pursuit of something. Rara makes a sweeping gesture in the direction of the island, which goes beyond the coconut palms. Mémé clucks and imitates him. They turn toward the dear gods, and with precipitate words, explain something very important to them. The boy's finger repeatedly brushes the fetishistic bracelet, while the girl's points to the design on the officer's wrist.

To what extent their speech expresses an idea that it is necessary to grasp, or merely constitutes a kind of collective birdsong, would be very difficult for the young people to discern. They only recognize a few syllables scattered here and there in the undulating chant. One name recurs—that of Kroum—and another that signifies the ancestor, the father. Those names the children articulate with increasing frequency, insistently, and with a sort of anxiety—which, there is no doubt about it, degenerates into interrogation...

To calm him down, Laurette draws the boy toward her, and repeats to him in an amicable tone: Yes, Rara, yes, Kroum...yes, the Ancestor."

A radiance of delight lights up in the children's eyes. They clap their hands, jumping for joy, expanding in a dizzying flood of speech.

Laurette smiles. "Do you understand any of this, Hugues?"

Hugues shakes his head. "I think you've just made our friends a promise."

"I don't know what," Laurette says, "but it will be necessary to keep it. You'll help me..."

Darkness falls. The officer and the young woman return to the beach. A great gentle weariness overwhelms Laurette. She squeezes her cousin's hand and retires to her tent.

Raramémé lie down across the threshold. They can still be heard chatting in whispers. Then they snuggle together and go to sleep, entwined, like two kittens.

The *Citoyen*'s carpenters are plying the ax, the saw, the plane and the mallet relentlessly. Thanks to the wood with which the island is overflowing, the few necessary repairs are easy to effectuate. Decorated with the scars of her exploit, the light cruiser will be in a fit state to regain her fatherland, but it is heavy work and it is necessary that her sojourn is a long one. Only Monsieur Bedeau-Conflans and his secretary are genuinely annoyed by that.

The delay permits the delegate, it is true, to complete the general report of his mission. But Monsieur Pittagol, to whom that responsibility falls, would just as soon carry it out in his apartment in the Rue du Bac. And for long weeks, the Chambre will have been deprived of the eloquence and labor of one of the leaders of the radical-democratic party. How much more prejudicial that absence is at a time when political unease is increasing, and a ministerial crisis might perhaps permit a new man to take the helm!

The député has difficulty consoling himself for that inconvenience. The company of kangaroos, ornithorhynchi and even that of all the varieties of psittacoids leaves him unsatiated. The indigenes only catch occasional glimpses of the horizons of democracy. On the orders of his employer, Monsieur Pittagol spends every evening around the hearth, promoting their civic education.

Certainly, the song of the little hairy sorcerer is listened to with docility. Varied and picturesque dances accompany the session, and the words of the Elders are full of deference, but Monsieur Pittagol does not grasp many of them, and he has become convinced that his audience does not understand any of his. Although that particularity scarcely differentiates the Oyas from the conscientious proletariat that haunts electoral meetings and popular universities, it does not stimulate his zeal—and he sinks into the melancholy mood into which his incurably wounded heart is sliding.

For Monsieur Pittagol is in love, and his love is in vain. Is the colonial officer the lover of the frail young blonde? Contrary to the opinion amidships, Monsieur Pittagol doubts it—but there is a cordial and banal relationship between them. She has given the officer, if not her body, the most precious part of her heart—and the surplus belongs to two Polynesian brats and an ape. That preference ulcerates and humiliates Monsieur Pittagol. He can only ease his pain by indulging in compassion for it.

Monsieur Pittagol soothes himself by distilling abstruse prose pieces and amorphous verses in which he curses his slavery.

If Commandant Kerfaouët did the same, he might gnaw less impatiently at his leash, but he is irritated. The

Citoyen's exploit has opened up a fine prospect of promotion; what bad luck it is to be immobilized in this lax Cytherea—all the more so because the atmosphere is not conducive to rigorous orders. A humane and conscientious leader, Monsieur de Kerfaouët feels an obligation not to begrudge young men whose lives are hanging by a thread the interval of relief that hazard has accorded them. In rotation, the men have permission to go ashore until eight o'clock in the evening; they savor the island's pleasures with intoxication.

Monsieur de Kerfaouët has been obliged to impose certain restrictions. In order not to injure the forbearance of the Oyas, who do not immolate game for everyday consumption and who asks its forgiveness, he has limited hunting permits severely. The sailors have not protested. Big children, they take little joy in massacring trusting beasts and, instead of killing them, are gladly exerting their ingenuity in domesticating them. In imitation of the savages, some have adopted one species, others another. Lancosme has appointed himself patron of armadillos; the loquacious Loustau that of the discreet kiwis; Balissard from Ménilmuche is so well-viewed by Pippi-kuink that if it continues, Raramémé will be jealous. Even though people joke about it, Châtenet has become the intimate of the white-maned macaques that roost in the coconut palms.

Naturally, this familiarity does not extend as far as Kouang. One day, when they were a little drunk, two or three of the lads attempted to tease him; they received such shoves that the joke has not been repeated. Half out of respect and half in jest, when they cross his limping path, they render him honors. "No one will ever make me believe, old chap, that the fellow doesn't know a lot more than he lets on."

The most cordial relations have been stabilized with the indigenes. They have maintained the traditions of generous hospitality that won the affection of the navigators of the eighteenth century. One cannot say, since they have none, that their hearths are open to the white gods, but in the appropriate measure, the latter are at home in the company of all. The women smile at them and open their arms. Jealousy is unknown to the husbands. What Amphitryon would not rejoice in sharing with Jupiter?

In the midst of these exotic idylls, the sailors have forgotten the perils that they have recently escaped. Those of tomorrow? Wait and see. Homesickness has ceased to gnaw at them. The seductive, alluring atmosphere impregnates them. An alcoholic beverage extracted from palm juice does not taste bad, and renders them more profound and more comforting dreams.

In Oaleya the Fortunate, Hugues de Pionne and Laurette stroll untiringly, rediscovering the soul of their childhood. In this climate, where almost the entire race is afflicted by the same malaise as her, the young woman savors a respite, a wellbeing forgotten for years. She no longer has a fever. She eats with appetite. She sleeps, and wakes up refreshed in the cool morning. Often, she and Hugues set off at dawn. Raramémé take charge of a few provisions. They remain absent all day.

Within a radius of several kilometers, all the charms of the exquisite island are now familiar to them. Nowhere, save for the old ancestral house, has such an amicable and reassuring atmosphere ever surrounded them.

There are no dangerous animals on the island. Even the snakes here are harmless. Houga and Lauritea are the friends of all species. As they approach, the kangaroos lift up their timid muzzles amicably, and the armadillos no longer take the trouble to enclose themselves in their scaly boxes. The cackle of the parrots welcomes them, and the monkeys, anticipating some treat, would become indiscreet if Raramémé were not alert. Kiwi escorts them gravely, accompanied by his female and little ones.

They are now familiar with a host of delightful, ardent, moving locations.

They are acquainted with the lagoon with the thick waters full of ferments, around which an immense swirl of spirits circulates. They are acquainted the other lagoon with the clear waters, where the incessantly-oscillating crowns of the great acacias are mirrored. They are acquainted with the two forests of coconut-palms, one of bananas, and the enormous thickets of mulberries and guavas, beneath the somber vaults of the forked mango-trees.

They are familiar with Kouang's grotto.

Barefoot, they have gone up the stream of the little river, visited the fissures where the skeletons of the great extinct birds sleep.

Guided by the children, they have also made other discoveries. They have gone with them as far as the vicinity of Hakarou, the volcano. As one approaches it the vegetation becomes stunted, dries out and disappears. There is nothing but a bare ground of lava and sulfur, which creaks bizarrely underfoot, quivering, snoring and becoming hot. A stink fills the air. Encircled by charred earth, pools of water and oily mud seethe, in which bubbles burst. Unbreathable vapors scatter filthy spirits. Beneath the crust of the ground, others grunt like pigs. Miry and scalding geysers spring forth with enormous gouts of smoke. Everywhere there are ashes, scoria and lava, quivering and anguished. Beneath it all, the enchained demons of a prodigious becoming agitate.

Another time, there was an even longer excursion. Raramémé led their friends to the southern tip of the island. It is terminated by a bluff, lashed by winds, an extremely high and sheer cliff that overlooks the sea vertically. There, colossal figures lie on their backs, like the sarcophagi of giants. Their feet are directed southwards, their immutable eyes staring into the sky. They are carved with a measure of skill, reminiscent of Phoenicia or Assyrian sculptures. The artists who created them were infinitely superior to the Oyas, who, apart from the traditional designs of totems, reproduced indefinitely according to a rigorous and invariable perfection, seem to be almost strangers to the fine arts.

How were the masses of these stone gods transported? By whom? What is their significance? An unfathomable mystery. Raramémé have explained that, apart from the ancestor Manga-Yaponi, no other members of the tribe would dare to contemplate them, except on sacred days, but that the four of them can, since they are children of the crab.

The children have also shown the visitors the somber thickets in which Minniloa, the Black Flower, grows. Dr. Boujade, who has accompanied them, has explained its properties to them. Those who are tired of life innocently request a peaceful end from it. Hugues sniggered: "Tell that to Monsieur Bedeau-Conflans. Death without tears—what an export!"

Pensively, Laurette looked up at the young man and placed a finger on his lips. "You mustn't say anything. It would be too dangerous."

On another occasion, Raramémé, cutting a path through the tall grass and lianas, take their friends to a strange clearing. A dome of interlaced foliage covers it, in which white and red corollas blossom that are almost monstrous. The ground is carpeted with soft and tenuous moss sprinkled with silver flowers. It is bordered on one side by Taroa, the dormant waters of which are swarming with turtles, frogs, insects, larvae, fish and eels. Such heady perfumes impregnate it that moisture forms on the temples and a kind of mist veils the brain. A breath passes through it, powerful, warm and sweet, like the caress of a velvet wing. Gripped by vertigo, Laurette feels herself become unsteady, and lets herself fall unwittingly on to Hugues' shoulder.

Watching the couple with a tender and very cheerful gaze, Raramémé explain things, self-importantly. Intrigued, the young couple, wanting to understand, appeal to Monsieur Boujade for help. He knows more words than they do, and grasps their connections more fully. He listens attentively, makes an effort, and suddenly bursts out laughing.

Laurette interrogates him. He avoids the issue.

She insists, eventually becoming annoyed.

Then, satirically, he says: "At your own risk, Madame. Anyway, since you're children of the crab, you won't be scandalized. You're not unaware that the entire island is full of spirits. Our little friends move in an invisible world that has as much reality for them as my shoe or that flying squirrel spying on us over there in the fork of that mango-tree. Now, know that this place full of saps and odors is simmering, if I might put it like that, the magma of what will be. Here, you and the captain are going to impregnate yourselves with the most alluring perfumes and germs…with the result that, if the will of Rahuo intervenes, in nine months, the people of the crab will be enriched by a new recruit—to whom, Madame, you will give birth."

Laurette blushes and bursts out laughing. "How silly!"

The afternoons rarely end without a visit to the village. Of all the white gods, those of the crab are the tribe's favorites. They pause in front of the huts, pronounce words that augur well, touch the sick, distribute candy to the children, glass beads to the women and smiles to everyone. Then, heaped with blessings, they descend to the beach of golden sand, and there, with Raramémé playing at their feet, facing the setting sun, the smoking volcano, the purring waves and the black coral, they savor peace, melancholy and acceptance.

Everything is finishing, everything crumbling, including dolor. Nothing is entirely bad. Almost everything is good. Everything is good, since nothing endures...

And very often, the evening ends with the rhythmic canticle of the crabs. Hougalauritea have learned the tune and the words now; they know how to intone it in the necessary fashion. Their voices and those of the savage children rise up in chorus. It is sufficient for them to call; in a few moments, the fraternal animality surges from the Ocean and surrounds them.

Lost in the swarming life that envelops them, the young couple experience a bizarre sensation of comfort and delight. Everything was a dream, save for the children they once were, and whom they have rediscovered, and the strange games that have revived within them, across the generations, the emprise of the unknown Ancestor.

It is evident that Raramémé have a project, with which they want to associate Hougalauritea. They raise it agitatedly, on a daily basis, with great speeches and abundant gestures. Unfortunately, it is difficult to grasp. It seems to be a matter of an excursion to be made together. It will be necessary to traverse the whole island, probably to spend one or two nights in the forest, and visit something.

What?

Summoned to consultation, Dr. Boujade has declared himself impotent to clarify the enigma. Probably a taboo place, a sanctuary, or more images of a magical character, like the colossi of the southern promontory.

Invariably, at the end of their speeches, the children never fail to designate the totem inscribed on their breast and on the wrists of the young couple, and the name of Kroum returns to their lips with vivacity. There is no doubting the interest of the trip, which is presumably connected with the indigenes' superstitions, and will lift a further corner of the veil of the unknown that envelopes them.

In vain Hugues raises objections, fearing that it might be too tiring for Laurette. She is strong and alert. She has never felt better.

"We're leaving tomorrow, Doctor. Would you like to come with us?"

For form's sake, Monsieur Boujade demurs. In truth, what need do the two young folk have of him? Nevertheless the bonhomie that he hides beneath his playful Southern skepticism is touched; his curiosity also scents an appetizing mystery. Then again, to flee, to flee for forty-eight hours, the new obsession that has taken hold of the Delegate General: could Oaleya not become a kind of sanitarium for the sick and wounded of his constituency? Monsieur Boujade is required to assemble the meteorological documentation. With a thermal bath and a little summer-house... The capital will not be difficult to find.

At dawn, escorted by the brown children and the Hairy One, the excursionists set out. They plunge delightedly into the forest, powdered with dew and overflowing with perfumes.

It is forbidden for the sailors to go more than three kilometers from the camp. Nonchalant, finding without difficulty in their immediate vicinity all that they need for their subsistence, slaves of the instinct that engages them to remain grouped together, the indigenes hardly ever go beyond the same radius. Hougalauritea and their companions have the gigantic forests, the babbling streams, the still pools, the shady valleys and the abrupt escarpments entirely to themselves.

At the departure, distractedly, the young woman has enquired: "Have any new communications come in?" And then, the wireless known and forgotten, they have abandoned themselves to the dazzling delight of the Garden of Eden of which they are the privileged guests.

Raraméмé precede them, brush against them and follow them, dancing around with the petulance of young mad dogs. They are scouts, supporters, providers and rearguard. They are perpetually running up, their hands laden with presents: orchids with surprising corollas, fruits, calabashes, clusters of grapes, beetles with polished metal wing-cases, a ruby butterfly or a little bird, a warm living gem plucked from its nest—and which, after having brushed it with her lips, Laurette releases into the air.

The brown children wrestle with one another, chase one another, knock one another over, roll around, bite one another. Kouang sometimes plays his part. Climbing after him through the trees, leaping from branch to branch, they bombard him with coconuts, challenge him, abuse him. He ends up losing his patience, turns round, launches himself with a prodigious agility, catches up with the tormentors, takes hold of them, shakes them, swings them from the end of his arms. They utter shrill cries, burst out laughing, escape and pester him even harder. The frightened macaques scatter and the multi-colored parrots fly away with strident protests.

The midday halt takes place in the depths of a verdant valley, beneath the vast crowns of lataniers, near a small waterfall streaming in a casket of somber plush. Sheltered from the ardent sun, there is a humid and gentle coolness. Water-moles yawn on the moss. The shiny muzzle of an otter emerges, its eyes sparkling. It gazes briefly, and dives again, unhurriedly.

Is it certain that life could not have been modeled on another plan? Oh, a less abnormal development of the cerebral lobes, a less jealous individualism, a less bitter competition between creatures...

Laurette murmurs: "Hugues, how can we live anywhere else?"

The officer's lips contract, bitterly pursed. What! Is Laurette forgetting that this is the final halt? No, she knows. But she is resolutely proscribing and suppressing the universal anguish. And as if she believed it, she sketches plans.

"It's decided. We'll come back, when the war is over, to settle in Oaleya. Will you accompany us, Monsieur Boujade?"

Monsieur Boujade nods his head. "Be careful that we aren't to numerous. The other evening, I heard a group of sailors exchanging reflections. One said: 'Old chap I'm going to naturalize myself here after the war.' And another, a Basque, even sniggered: 'Good—me, I won't wait that long, and the *Citoyen* can leave without me.'"

Idle words. But can they escape the dissolving contagion of the magical isle? Might they not consent to stop playing their part in the universal martyrdom? Are they not allowing themselves, a trifle criminally, to be lulled, distracted, numbed?

The captain stiffens himself. "As the *Citoyen* won't leave without us, I propose that we get moving again."

The slope becomes steep. Doubtless they are approaching the culminating point of the island. The vegetation becomes stunted, almost disappearing. They follow a sinuous gorge that plunges between two walls, a chaos of stones where nothing grows but a few mosses and fleshy plants, among which snakes a thin trickle of water. Inoffensive—but sometimes enormous—lizards watch them pass by, stupidly. There is a cave on the left; its depths are invisible. It exhales a cold draught. At intervals, the defile contracts so narrowly between overhanging rocks that the sky becomes invisible.

Raramémé's petulance has evaporated. They approach the white gods, squeeze their hands and sing a muted alternating melody. Rara initiates, and Mémé takes up the refrain. Jealous demons make their abode here, which it is dangerous to disturb. Raramémé rarely apologize; it is not an unconsidered curiosity that is driving them. Over a distance, the call of the Great Ancestor has reached them. They are obeying, bringing the pale gods who are of the same blood.

A bizarre granitic pyramid looms up, like a prehistoric monolith. The children kneel at its base, cupping their hands. An unintelligible murmur emerges from their lips. A particularly redoubtable spirit must reside here. Raramémé turn round, pointing at their two companions, prostrating themselves more urgently.

Dr. Boujade conjectures: "I think our guides are asking the local Cerberuses for permission for us to pass."

"May it be granted!" says Madame de Vesnage, with a smile. And with the same gesture as the children, she extends her waxy palm toward the unknown gods, rings gleaming on her excessively thin fingers.

Raramémé get up, clicking their tongues. The affair is arranged. All is well. Forward ho! The rocky walls diminish. An almost desolate plateau, where the wind is bitter, is quickly crossed. The direction of a trickling stream of water indicates that the dividing line has been crossed. The excursionists accompany it, descending a series of terraces alongside it.

The vegetation is reborn. Here is the tall bracken again, and then the immense forest, overflowing with life, essences and odors. Under its vault, the air is embalmed, becoming deliciously lukewarm again.

The young woman feels a little tired. In the shelter of giant coconut-palms, in the midst of hibiscus bushes dotted with scarlet corollas and gardenias powdered with snow, a spring wells up, surrounded by divans of verdure.

"Shall we spend the night here?"

It is agreed. The children have understood, and approve the plan. They help the officer and the doctor prepare the bivouac. Dr. Boujade takes from his pocket the ardent little god enclosed therein, and causes the lightning to spring forth whose flame devours twigs. Raramémé clap their hands. Kouang blinks, approaches, crouches down and offers his formidable palms to the fire.

The children and the ape have collected oranges, mangoes and walnuts. Combined with the provisions brought in bags, it is a frugal but adequate supper. Beyond the crowns of the trees, the stars twinkle. The birds have gone to sleep. There is no longer anything but the furtive sounds and the immense sigh of the living forest.

Enveloped in a plaid blanket, the young woman is stretched out on a clump of moss and foliage. Slightly torpid, she contemplates the silhouettes of the two men sitting beside the fire, who are chatting in low voices while smoking. To one side, Kouang's mass is folded up.

Close to her, nestled together, Raramémé are twittering softly. It is not a conversation. It is the new song that they have picked up while following the trail, and which is springing necessarily from their lips.

They are finally coming, with those who had to come. It has been a long time, but that is not their fault. Kroum has spoken, Kroum is alive.

Suddenly, Rara gets up, places his slender finger on his breast, then on Mémé's, goes to touch the officer's wrist, and the amulet suspended from the young woman's. He sits down again and explains to Laurette in a coaxing voice: "You and him. And me and her. Tomorrow, the four. And the Ancestor. Kroum is alive."

What does he mean?

The young woman asks Dr. Boujade. He is still perplexed. "It seems to be a matter of some family festival. Not being a member of the clan, I'm afraid of being indiscreet."

Laurette reassures him: "We invited you."

And then the silence, the great silence, thickens again. From the suave night, divine powers of appeasement well up. Through the dome of foliage the softness of the stars radiates, and the serenity of centuries streams.

A poor petty bloody rag ceases her solitary suffering. The immense collective pity embraces her, bandages her, coddles her. The shadow is warm with spare tenderness, caressing hands, smiling lips. A paternal benediction floats, reassures, protects, envelops. Everything menacing is far away, impotent. All is well. There is nothing true but acceptance. From the abysms of space and time, gleams emerge.

What are you, ungraspable images of dreams, surged from what millenarian gulfs, what limbos, what worlds beyond, ornamented with I know not what radiation?

One might think that they are shrunken visages of light. They are pitiful and amicable. They do not resemble anything on earth, but are ineffably reassuring. They are new. They are the same.

Are they not, in an old house on the other side of the world, grouped around a cradle? Are they not murmuring forgotten things that have returned? A subtle mist drowns hem, blurs them, dissimulates their features, attenuates their words, which, one divines, are so soft...

They pass by, return, hide away.

Oh! what a shiver, in sensing them approach again. Have they no names? No, undoubtedly...

No? Truly? Oh! that one, leaning over, whose blue eyes suddenly shine, illuminating the white forehead, in which the energetic and cheerful mouth is slightly parted....

Laurette utters a plaint of inarticulate joy, holds out her arms, stammers: "The Uncle of the Crabs..."

The children shiver, raise their heads. She makes an instinctive gesture, summoning them. They get up, approach, touch the face of the sleeper with their little hands, and nestle beside her, cheek to cheek.

She goes back to sleep, surrounded by the warmth of the two small bodies, which have the scent of the forest and gazelles.

En route, at dawn! *En route!* Scarcely has the sun winked between the black trunks than Raramémé are on their feet, shaking themselves, pawing the ground, twittering, running around.

There is a fury of movement in them, the delight of a bloodhound on a fresh trail. If the others took heed of them they would leave right away, immediately, without breakfast, without packing up their things.

Be bold... Be quick...

Laurette shares their impatience, scolding the slowness of her companions. "Come on, Doctor, aren't you ready? Remember that dawdling might perhaps cause to miss prodigious surprises."

Finally, the bags are buckled. Without hesitation, heads in the air, at a rapid pace, Raramémé set off. Laurette, nimbly, is at their heels. Her cheeks are rosy, her eyes shining. She is bounding. One might think that the children's excitement has infected her.

Hugues scolds her gently: "Calm down—you're going to make yourself ill."

She reassures him: "Have no fear. The god that our little friends have evoked is within me. And in addition, I sense that we're getting close to our goal."

The forest is reduced and thins out. Raramémé sniff the air and make signs. There it is—the odor of the sea. It insinuates itself, sharpens. Incessantly, the children chirp, turn round, gesticulate.

There is no doubt. They are getting close.

The curtain of the final trees has been passed. Here is a grassy plateau. The great breeze of the Pacific lashes their faces. In front of the excursionists there is a gentle slope, and then a promontory rises up above the immense swell of the waves. It is only covered by meager brushwood, patched here and there by a few clumps of bushes crowned by trees.

Raramémé stop momentarily, breathe deeply, sniff, mutter to one another, and, making signs bidding their companions to wait for them, begin describing curves, zigzags, circuits and interchanges. Their fingers extend feverishly, clench, wander from their faces to the breasts, and their lips emit a jerky chant:

> Ho? Ha? Hey hey!
> This way? That way?
> They're going…see?
> To you…to me?
> Oh! your ear is twitching!
> Tell me, nose, are you itching?
> Halt! Let's run…there's a sound
> My eye, your eye, look around…
> Boldly, jump high!
> The unknown is nigh!
> Now I know the score,
> It's not there any more
> Everything is troubled!
> The dark is redoubled.
> But way over there,
> In the far somewhere,
> Did something shimmer
> Is there a glimmer?
> It's him! The Ancestor!
> Greetings, great quester!

Be bold, still!
Hurrah, we will!

Raramémé, their eyes bright with joy, return to the young woman at a run, each of them grabbing one of her hands. Quickly, quickly, they run down the slope with her. The men have difficulty keeping up.

"Gently, kids!" Monsieur Boujade complains.

They have to slow down to force their way through the waist-high grass, which is becoming thicker, and then to go uphill for a hundred meters. A thicket surges forth to the height of a man. Kouang plunged into it, clearing a path...

A clearing...

An exclamation of surprise escapes all their mouths simultaneously.

Beneath the parasol of swaying coconut-palms, the skeleton of a hut is completing the process of crumbling away. It is not the one of the savages' huts. It is more reminiscent of a traditional peasant's cabin in one of our provinces—but everything is antiquated and falling apart. It no longer has a roof. The ruined walls are covered with climbing plants.

What does this unexpected apparition signify? Has some European been shipwrecked...?

"Let's go in," the captain says. "Perhaps there's a clue..."

He takes a step forward.

The children interpose themselves, however, stopping him. No, no, this is not the objective. Laurette joins them.

"Soon, Hugues. First, let's allow our little guides to take us where they wish."

Raramémé have taken their friend's hands again. Now they are passing through a final hedge of brushwood. There is a mound in front of them, which, at the highest point of the bluff, overlooks the ocean. The basalt there seems to be bare. But what seizes and stupefies all gazes is the prodigious thing that stands upon it.

Ineptly and primitively constructed, a coral cross extends its arms over a small elongated swelling.

"A grave! A European grave!"

The men take off their hats. Madame de Vesnage puts her fingers to her forehead and her breast. The children watch her. With a careful awkwardness, they imitate her gesture, crouching down on their heels, swaying back and forth, and intoning a guttural chant:

> Tick, tock,
> Clock, shock,
> Blood will arrive!
> Kroum is alive!
> Rahuo is the crab and the great Name
> Atua sleeps in the blue sky
> The crab is born of the sea's sigh
> From blue waves the Ancestor came
> And here are those who had to come
> To the summons of Rahuo's drum.
> Tick, tock,
> Clock, shock
> Blood has arrived,
> Kroum is alive!

Three times the two brown children get up, and then prostrate themselves, placing their foreheads on the coral slab.

The newcomers draw nearer to the cross, examining it anxiously. And all of a sudden, simultaneously, Hugues and Laurette bend down, uttering an exclamation: "The sign!"

In spite of the corrosion of time, there can be no mistake. Here, a careful artist has inscribed the same emblem that is engraved on the children's breasts, which Hugues bears on his wrist and which is suspended from Laurette's: a great crab, of the blue crab species of Polynesia, is minutely carved into the calcareous substance.

"What does it…?" stammers the young woman—but the words expire on her lips. Above the totem, other imprints are hollowed out, also recognizable, and perhaps even more unexpected. They are two letters of the European alphabet. There is an L and a V.

"Hugues," says Laurette, going pale. "An L... A V…"

What mad thought goes through their minds? The crab... An L... A V...

As pale as his cousin, the officer, the officer passes his hand over his forehead.

"Laurette, I beg you, don't get overexcited…"

The young woman's eyes are searching avidly. She utters a cry, and kneels down. At the foot of the cross, fragments of coral and rock are heaped up. Something is shining in the interstices.

In a matter of seconds, a wooden box encircled by iron is disengaged. It is an object of European manufacture, very old. Half-effaced ornaments are in the style of the eighteenth century. On the lid there is a metal plate, which reproduces the two letters L and V. From one of the carved metal projections, a key is suspended. It no longer turns in the rusted keyhole, but pressure suffices to make the old lock yield. The lid is raised.

The interior is lined with leather. No damp has penetrated. Laurette's tremulous fingers feel an antique fabric of silk brocade, and unfold it. It is a uniform, with a small épée. The cross of Saint Louis is attacked to the jacket. The young woman's teeth chatter. There must be something more...

Rara and Mémé are still swaying back and forth, continuing to sing:

The crab is born of the sea's frame
From blue waves the Ancestor came
And here are those who had to come
To the summons of Rahuo's drum.

There is something more. There is a large portfolio, in crimson morocco leather, marked with the same initials—but this time, beneath them, a coat of arms has been imprinted in the leather: arms that Hugues and Laurette recognize at first glance. They are inscribed on the bezel of the ring that the officer is wearing on his little finger, and on the antique brooch that the young woman is wearing at her neck. In the distant family dwelling in the Basque country, they subsist on parchments that lie dormant in the bottom of drawers, on pieces of silverware, on fragments of faience plates and chipped glassware.

By virtue of what fantastic combination of circumstances do they mark the grave and remains of a dead man?

Who, then, is the dead man?

Who?

Crazy as the coincidence is, Hugues and Laurette have put a name to him, even before the trembling young woman has succeeded in unfolding the yellowed

sheets of paper that she had just taken out of their enve-
lope. Large 18th-century handwriting covers them—the
same handwriting that sprawls over so many notebooks
piled out back there, in the antiquated cupboards that
smell of lavender, with collections of drawings, maps, a
few desiccated animal-skins, and seashells.

"The Uncle..."

Hugues and Laurette sit down side by side. Piously,
they open and read the testament of Luc de Vesnage,
captain of the king's armies, Chevalier de Saint Louis,
companion of Monsieur de La Pérouse, presumed to
have died with him, but whose remains and last will are
here:

Oaleya, in the Pacific Ocean
At the antipodes of so-called civilized Europe

There is little chance that this document will fall into the hands of any human being capable of deciphering
it. That is, in any case, the most sincere of my wishes. If
I am writing it, therefore, it is more for the satisfaction
of my mind than any other purpose. I wish with all my
might that vivifying putrefaction, in which even the
rocks that will cover them will end up, will simultaneously dilute and absorb all the other traces of my existence.

It pleases me, however, before returning to dissolve
in the great All, to make use of the means that civilization once conferred upon me to record a few reflections
and consign the testimony of my gratitude to this privileged region of the globe, where, for more than thirty-
three years—my whim has kept a meticulous calendar of
the seasons and the days—I have enjoyed a felicity of

which I had never previously glimpsed any image on the earth.

It was on the fourteenth of January 1782 that the frigate *Astrolabe*, bearing the flag of Monsieur de La Pérouse, was constrained by some slight damage to drop anchor off the coast of this island, which the indigenes call Oaleya. I had succeeded in joining the expedition in order to complete the research in natural history that has been the great curiosity of my life, and also to see at close range the primitive populations of which Messieurs Cook and Bougainville have reported so many admirable things. The extreme disgust that a half-century of experience had led me to conceive for the mass of ignominies that we designate by the name of civilization caused me to attach an exceptional price to the second category of studies.

It required some time for me to convince myself that hazard had served me better than could reasonably have hoped. And if I were not an atheist, I would recognize the hand of God in the extraordinary combination of circumstances that has led me to the only place in the world where the dream that has haunted me for so many years has been realized.

Having consigned contemporary Europe to execration, quarreled with all the members of my family, abjured all the prejudices of my class, my spirit only found some appeasement in the sublime discourses in which Monsieur Rousseau, Monsieur Raynal[20] and Monsieur

---

[20] Guillaume Thomas Raynal (1713-1796) compiled and published the four-volume *Histoire philosophique et politique des établissements et du commerce des Européens dans les deux Indes* (1770), with substantial contributions by Diderot and Holbach; it became a key document of the Enlightenment be-

de Migurac,[21] the gentleman philosopher, and a few other men of genius have demonstrated to us that, low as humankind has fallen, it was not fatally avowed to evil, and that only lamentable errors had precipitated it into Gehenna.

I nourished the obstinate hope that perhaps, somewhere, preferably at the antipodes, innocent populations, protected from our corruption by distance and by circumstances, were still living in the primitive purity of humanity. An inextinguishable thirst burned in me to join their school.

A few days sufficed to convince me that the naïve simplicity of the Oyas considerably surpassed what my most ambitious dreams had imagined. My project was, therefore, quickly conceived. Having secretly conveyed to land a small number of objects to which my memory was attached or which I feared that my weakness as a civilized man might render it uncomfortable for me to do without, I waited with an impatience that I concealed until the eve of the departure.

When I knew that it was irrevocably fixed for the next day's dawn, I wished Monsieur de La Pérouse and the ship's officers goodnight after supper and, in the middle of the night—which was, by a rare stroke of luck, exceedingly dark—I left my cabin, went up on deck, left my snuff-box there, threw my jacket, doublet and a few

cause of its strident championship of democracy. Although initially unsigned, the association of the text with its principal author could not be concealed, and he went into exile when the book was burned by the public executioner.

[21] One of Lichtenberger's quirkier early works was *Monsieur de Migurac ou le marquis philosophe* (1903), an account of the life and ideas of a fictitious Enlightenment philosopher.

objects that I thought capable of floating into the water, dived in silently after them, and reached land by swimming vigorously.

The following day, I had the inexpressible joy of seeing, from the top of a hill, that my stratagem had had the greatest success. No one aboard had doubted that I had drowned. The frigate raised anchor and set sail at the appointed hour.

It was thus that I became a guest of the Oyas. It was sufficient for me to reveal myself to those honest folk to be immediately admitted to the bosom of their virtuous community, to the mores of which I took care to accommodate myself scrupulously.

Having observed that each of them bore on the breast the figure of a sacred animal, I made the choice, on a whim, of the crab, my studies having been preferentially devoted to crustaceans of that variety. It happened that the animal in question, the features of which one of their artists engraved in my flesh, was that of their most illustrious clan. Thus, in the measure to which any inequality can exist among these simple children of nature, I found myself connected with their finest clan.

According to their custom, disdainful of all the prejudices that are the fruit of our egotism and our corruption, it was given to me to enter into the most pleasant relationship with a few of the women of the tribe, those most graciously modeled by nature. Thus I experienced the sensuality of innocent amours untroubled by the paltriness of our jealousy. Similarly, I knew the healthy joys of an abundant paternity. After a few years, the children of the crab, whose race had seemed to be on the brink of extinction when I arrived, enjoyed a new numerousness on the sunlit shores and among the cheerful arbors.

Will it be given to these people that the decline to which they seem doomed might be reversed? I dare not count on it. It cannot, however be doubted that Oaleya, in the ensemble of the created world, constitutes an anomaly that seems bound to disappear.

Here, humans live exempt from the deadly passions and pitiless necessities that have darkened their existence elsewhere. Here, they do not nurture the furious mania of property, aggressive egotism, the need to command and the instinct of combat. A prodigal Nature provides all their needs without their being subjected to the harsh law of labor. Cheerfully sharing the fruits that she offers to all, the Oyas have conserved the habits of confidence, friendship and fraternal generosity that have been replaced elsewhere by unsociability, envy and hatred. No Oya is fully happy save in the midst of the happiness of his fellows.

Alas, I cannot doubt that this adolescent regime is not within the present aims of pitiless destiny. In spite of the delightful climate that cradles them, and in spite of the simplicity of their mores, these natives have been attained by an implacable evil. As far as I can remember, I have had fourteen or fifteen spouses, who have all preceded me to the tomb, and of the forty or so children that have been accorded to us, more than half have already returned the spirit that animated them to the Unknown. Since my arrival in the fortunate isle, the population has been reduced by at least a quarter or a third, Undoubtedly, it does not enter into the plan of Providence that this intermediary link between atrocious wig-wearing humankind and unconscious animality will be preserved.

I am convinced that there are several other species of which individuals still subsist here that have already disappeared elsewhere. I have encountered, wandering languidly among the thickets, the last of the melancholy Moas, of which only the whitened bones remain today. Thus will disappear the ornithorhynchi, the kiwis, the armadillos and so many other singular beasts, indecisive sketches that Nature, having made her choice, has decided to destroy.

That our pride should persuade us that we and the animality we know, enslave and exploit have the prerogative any character of permanence is, however, irreconcilable with the weakness of creatures. I consider it certain that the furious appetite of humans to dominate the planet will gradually banish the majority of the beings that populate it. All those will be seen to disappear that are offend humans, that are inconvenient to them, the appetites of which require large spaces and abundant nourishment. I regard as already condemned the superb big carnivores, the great proboscidians, the paradoxical giraffes, and the strange tapirs. Other species will follow them to the tomb, and if humans go all the way to the conclusion of their vocation, they will end up as the sole masters of the globe, surrounded by slaves and beasts of burden.

However—thank God!—the murderous species carries the seeds of its own destruction within it. Its members will devour one another with their own teeth, will tear one another apart with their own claws, will poison one another with venoms that they cultivate internally. The species will take responsibility, with regard to itself, for executing the decrees on Nature, which prescribe perpetual annihilation and perpetual renaissance.

And it is, I am convinced, in the same crucible that will see the obsolete forms of the creature fade away and die that those of the future will be elaborated. Here, the fatalities demanding that we perish are ineluctably manifest. Here too, the equally-fatal resurrections are formidably manifest. In this embalmed atmosphere, in these thickets, marshes and river-banks, germs are pullulating. Even more prodigious are the powers of fecundity slumbering and seething in the oceans, from which all past lives have emerged.

Here, perhaps, like that of the giant birds, the innocent race of the Oyas will be extinct in a few hundred years. But I have discovered surprising vestiges of enigmatic creatures on their beaches. Perhaps, nearby, in the great depths, the masterpieces of animality that are yet to be are being sketched out. In the nameless debris and bizarre jellies that I have trampled underfoot in the sand in the wake of tempests, are the first lineaments of the Voltaires and Diderots of the day after tomorrow. I do not mean individuals, as we understand them, but the superior cells of the collective species, a hundred times superior to humans, which will succeed humans, and whose diffuse soul, glimpsed in advance by the simple Oyas in the multitude of spirits that they believe to be surrounding them, will far surpass our poor petty horizons, and will rise far above the Lilliputian successes of the spoiled pygmies and pretentious ants that we are.

Eternal God—no, Inconceivable Nature—thanks be rendered to you that here, for thirty years, sheltered from your traps, innocent of your crimes, I have known a peaceful existence, between the corals, the sea and the sky, among the least harmful of humans, learning to detach myself from the unhealthy and ridiculous egotism of ephemera, to nourish myself on the idea of permanence, and to consent, in scorning it, to your indefinite evolution.

Tomorrow, full of days and feeling my strength diminishing, I shall drink the Black Flower. I shall not wait for the decadence of senility to make a hideous wreck of me, clinging to the last flotsam of my shipwreck. I shall depart, an octogenarian patriarch, satiated with days, leaving behind me a numerous posterity, exempt from superfluous fears and vain hopes. It pleases me to be swallowed up by this gracious, perfumed earth, full of spirits, cradled by the murmurous sea, thinking that the atoms that made me will melt into it in order to be recombined here.

And it is not without a surge of gratitude for destiny that, on the brink of effacing myself, I turn one last time toward the unhappy Europe that I quit thirty years ago. King Louis XVI has doubtless terminated his monotonous reign and his successor, the young Louis XVII, is doubtless seeing the egotism of the privileged and the covetousness of the jealous poor conflict. Perhaps, to the internal dissensions of the State, external convulsions are added. Or perhaps—who knows?—after the fever whose tremors were felt, Europe might have gone back to sleep, in advance of centuries of torpor. No matter. Here, I have lived in accordance with the truth.

I am going to die.

In accordance with my instructions, the children of the crab will deposit my body in the grave that they will dig on the coral cape, near the cottage in which I was happy. In memory of my origins, I wanted a cross to designate my tomb. I am pleased that my body, covered worth earth, will dissolve there without being prey to beasts. In a carefully-sealed casket, I shall deposit these sheets of paper, along with the last objects connected with my sojourn among the civilized. I hope that this legacy, remaining inviolate, will slowly fall into impalpable dust.

My future brother, of whom I know so little, if hazard nevertheless permits you to unseal that stone and open this box, may this supreme advertisement of a dead man, who was almost as mad as you are, salute you and, at least, spare you from one crime.

Envy one of your peers who was able to remove his own existence from the general dementia of humankind and take from his example the resolution of imitating him to the extent that you can. If you are not able to do that, I adjure you, at least, if you have any compassion in your soul, to spare the innocent creatures who might perhaps still inhabit this locale.

Having read these lines, replace this message in the coffer that contains it, Reseal the coffer, bury it again underground, and, leaving this tomb behind you just as you found it, go away.

Go away and do not come back.

Forget it.

If a few Oyas are still alive, have pity on them. Do not commit the felony of attempting to convert them to civilization.

Go away. Leave them the pleasure of cradling themselves in their innocent dreams, thanks to which they have almost not been human, before becoming stones again, or—who knows?—ungraspable and inconceivable spirits, among which, perhaps, I shall be wandering tomorrow, a citizen of a world built on another plane than anything I am capable of imagining.

If you do that, my brother, receive the blessing of the man who lies here, May you go to sleep in the same peace as him, having had your fill of human beings, careless of gods, reconciled with unfathomable Nature, as disdainful of being as of nothingness!

I sign these pages with the name I bore among white men for fifty-three years:

Luc de Vesnage
18 June 1815

Hugues repeats: "18 June 1815—the day of Waterloo!"

Of the titanic epic that turned the world upside-down, Luc Vesnage lived and died as insouciant as he was of the work of the madepores and the courses of the stars.

Her eyes vague, Laurette stammers, in a wan, broken voice: "This is the Uncle, and this is his last adieu!"

Hugues inclines his head. Crouched at their feet, the brown children contemplate them with their tender and wild eyes. The officer adds: "And these, Laurette, really are our little cousins."

On the great earth, indifferent and foreign, these two savage children are the only living links that still connect them to their bloodline.

Dr. Boujade has moved away, discreetly, and is botanizing.

Kouang is dreaming, his gaze on the horizon.

They have reread the testament, rereading it slowly, line by line. The great Ocean is purring. The breeze is moaning. Vast albatrosses are soaring high overhead. Lower down, a few seagulls are exchanging shrill cries. There is a grave, powerful and serene peace. Yes, the Uncle of the Crabs has chosen a good place to die and rest.

The sun is already sinking, however. The shadows are spreading.

Hugues touches his cousin's arm. "It's getting late, Laurette. What do you want to do?"

She looks at him. "We have to obey."

"Obey?"

With her finger, the young woman indicates the open box. She makes a gesture.

He understands, but makes a suggestion: "We could wait until tomorrow."

She shakes her head negatively, reassembles the sheets of paper, tucks them into the leather portfolio and replaces them, with the folded clothes, in the box. They close it and, aided by the children, pile up the fragments of coral and stone on the lid. Now, everything is invisible, as it was when they arrived.

Then, for a second time, they kneel down at the foot of the mound, put their hands together and implore the mercy of the inconceivable God. When they have prayed in accordance with the ancestral rite, they make the sign of the cross.

And Raramémé, whose blood is the same as theirs, understand that it is necessary to associate themselves with that solemn action.

The two savages also kneel down, and similarly raise their brown paws to their foreheads and their breasts, participating in the invocation.

Papeiti has transmitted a cablegram from the Rue Royale.

Invite you, as soon as repairs are concluded, to return Toulon. By reason of political situation, presidential council deems extremely urgent return of Delegate General Bedeau-Conflans, whose communication unanimously appreciated by Chambre.

After having conferred with the député, Monsieur de Kerfaouët has replied:

Repairs completed. Preparing depart tomorrow. Delegate General puts his devotion at disposal of Republic.

Initially, Monsieur Pittagol had written "At disposal of Ministry," but Monsieur Bedeau-Conflans corrected him. The Ministry might fall; the Republic endures.

This is, therefore, the last day when the *Citoyen*'s passengers will tread the soil of the fortunate isle. The cruiser has taken aboard its full complement of fresh water, and loaded a cargo of fruits and roots. The fires are lit. The crew was ordered aboard two hours ago, except for the last service detachment.

It has required the amicable authority of the officers to prevent regrettable defections. The removal from the delightful island is cruel. Not everyone could tear himself away. Yesterday, under the mango-trees, the lifeless body of Balissard from Ménilmuche was found, lying beside that of young Tao-Hoaré. It was thought at first to have been a murder, but a rapid examination sufficed for Monsieur Boujade to falsify that hypothesis. Balissard had simply absorbed the Black Flower.

That is an example whose contagion is to be feared; congestion has been recorded as the cause of death, and it has been resolved to hasten the departure.

Even so, the cruiser cannot quit these waters without the representative of France addressing a few words of farewell to the population.

That afternoon, therefore, the indigenes are assembled on the beaten iron esplanade that separates the huts. The companions of the sailors, who have almost understood for some days what is going on, have informed the tribe. It is understood that the whale-mountain is going to disappear, with the white gods, and that it is appropriate to honor them one last time.

The Oyas have acquired a profound knowledge of their mores during recent weeks. The simple sailors are not much different from humans, save for the color of their skin, but the chiefs who have golden totems on their clothing and head-dresses are very powerful. Commandant Kerfaouët and the prophet with the tricolor belly are elevated above the rest.

Dr. Boujade disposes of mighty spells. He can make rain fall, swell the sea, extinguish the sun.

Captain de Pionne and the young woman owe a less fearful veneration to the sign of Kroum.

Everything that emanates from such gods must be respectfully received until the end. That is why, this afternoon, the entire population assembles, and they prostrate themselves three times with long howls when the député, his breast striped by his sash, stands up, takes a step forward, clears his voice, and, when silence is reestablished, intones his swan song.

"Citizens of Oaleya! This is the hour when the fatherland, still at grips with the infamous aggressor, is reclaiming me. I would be neglecting a very pleasant duty if, before quitting this hospitable island, I did not assure you of the total benevolence of the Republic.

"Ancient ties, the discovery of which has been very moving for us"—the orator bowed solemnly toward Laurette de Vesnage, who is very pale—"have linked our races for more than a century. The pious care with which you have honored the tomb of a Frenchman who was the precursor of the humanitarian ideals for which our fatherland is fighting today, attest to the ideal community that unites us, beneath differences of mentality.

"For three-quarters of a century the tricolor flag planted by one of the celebrated forebears or our commandant"—inclination of the head toward Monsieur de

Kerfaouët—"has been revered by you. Your diligent care, of which, when I return to France, I shall have the honor of rendering an account to my compatriots, who are yours, attest to the degree to which the free choice of your hearts has ratified our alliance. The Great War has given you an opportunity to furnish a new proof of your sentiments to the metropolis. Even in these peaceful regions, the monstrous barbarism of the Boche"—at this point, a snort in the orator's voice generated a frisson—"has been unleashed. Here, you have crushed it. The work commenced against the pirates by your rocks, your indomitable arms have completed.

"Here, the *U-37A* and its crew of pirates have found the punishment for their crimes. Why was it necessary for a premature death to steal from our affection the hero whom your suffrage designated to the government of the Republic to bear on his beast the glorious emblem that I was proud to pin upon him with my own hand? Let him remain an example for us. Lift up your hearts!"

At this declaration a band of macaws flies away and several women emit screeches of fright.

"I am departing for France, having taken an exact account of your aspirations and needs. I shall say over there that your devotion continues to be acquired by the motherland. In exchange, have no doubt that, on receipt of my report, she will show herself disposed to accord you an increasingly narrow participation in the gestation of our common destiny. I do not despair of soon seeing Oaleya, through the intermediary of a representative that she has freely chosen, making her voice heard in the harmonious chorus of the greater France of tomorrow!"

After all, who can foresee the whims of universal suffrage? An accident can happen quickly. In case of a metropolitan misadventure, Oaleya might be worth as much as Chandannagar or Martinique.

Translated by Monsieur Pittagol, the supreme song of the god is welcomed in a spirit of veneration and relief. Ungraspable as its substance is, there is no doubt that it is a song of adieu. That is the essential thing. The white gods have been merciful to the Oyas. They have not inflicted tortures upon them. They have brought them curious aliments, exquisite liquids, and amiable amours. They have been content with a single murder and have not seemed to demand others. It is appropriate to thank them for that.

So, Manga-Yaponi, swaying his white head, intones delightedly the canticle of gratitude.

"Redoubtable gods, be blessed for having spared us. We prostrate ourselves before your faces and beg you to take all your magic away with you. We shall continue to honor your signs. Try not to come back, for you make us very afraid and our minds are exhausted by the perpetual apprehension of not understanding you. Nevertheless, whatever you decide, we shall always be submissive to you. We have immediately killed the victim of your choice, and if another is necessary to you, we will kill them similarly, even if it is a hunter in the prime of life or a plump maiden. The important thing is that you go away without anger at your slaves."

A unanimous moan confirms the devotion of the tribe.

Monsieur Pittagol gives evidence of his indefatigable enthusiasm. Deeply moved, the député bows and proclaims, on straightening up: "*Vive la République! Vive la France!*"

At that liberating gesture, delight burst forth. The god is not demanding more blood. There is a single howl: *"Biba Ulica! Biba Francea!"*

With the masculine voice of the député, who intones the *Marseillaise*, the voices of all the little spouses who have profited from the patriotic instruction of the sailors join in with touching good will. It is, unfortunately impossible, for want of having made the discovery, to follow it with the national anthem of the Oyas—but when the choirs fall silent, a furious concert of irritated macaques and cockatoos is unleashed in the coconut-palms.

The session ends.

One after another, the launches have returned to the ship, with the député, the Commandant, his officers and their escort.

No one remains ashore except the young couple and Dr. Boujade. They have obtained permission from Monsieur de Kerfaouët for the last boat not to take them back until nightfall.

On the beach of golden sand, in the glory of the setting sun, a poignant bite grips the young woman and the officer.

At the moment of quitting the fortunate isle, Laurette weakens, rebels.

What? Stay? Desert the duty of the civilized that the old family tradition has inculcated within them? Not for a second, any more than in the strict conscience of the young officer, has the thought entered her head. On the plane on which they have lived, their lives are pledged; they will pay.

On being torn away from this place, however, the grief surpasses what she believed herself to be capable of suffering. How can she live, having broken the new links that have just revealed her to herself, become embodied in her own substance?

Yes, she was able, once, to drag out the days, alone, astray, abandoned in horror.

She cannot do that any longer.

Here, she has not only lived heart to heart with the man she loves, but their being has been enlarged, magnified beyond terrestrial infirmity in a prodigious communion.

They are not only beloved with all the poor tenderness of the hearts of a man and a woman; it is the entire race of which they are the issue that is beloved in them, that has ornamented their love with all that exists of aspiration toward the best, of hatred for evil and ugliness.

They are loved with all the humanitarian idealism of the Uncle of the Crabs, with all the innocence that palpitates in infantile souls, with all the desire for happiness of a creature seeking desperately to surpass the fatalities that grip it.

Raised above themselves, extracted from their individualism and from the universal carnage, they have, in the bosom of the fortunate isle, participated in the rhythm of a finer, superior, broader existence, as fraternal as the two savage children who foresaw their coming, who were waiting for them, who have recognized them, and have provided their bonds of union with immense Nature.

Break with all that? But that is as criminal as breaking with the old fatherland would be on the other plane. To desert the island and to desert France: equal impossibilities...

What to do, then?

Huddled at the young woman's feet, Raramémé watch her curiously, collecting on their brown fingers and licking off, on by one, the salty pearls that trickle down her cheeks.

Laurette wrings her hands and indicates the children.

"Help me, Doctor. Have pity. We can't abandon them."

Monsieur Boujade shrugs his shoulders, and grumbles, hiding his emotion behind a joke: "Nothing simpler than to take them aboard. Two marmosets more or less... For them, the cage, the asphalt of our streets, costumes from Belle Jardinière, bronchitis, the comfort of the hospital and the dissecting-table...fine gifts. Not much fun."

Laurette weeps.

Hugues murmurs in her ear: "Don't we have to be sensible, darling? The Uncle...we'll be leaving our dear bronze children in the embalmed atmosphere where they've flourished, among familiar spirits, in the perfumed light where life is sweet, memory without anguish, death without terror. They'll wait for us...and when the war is over, we'll come back..."

Through the mist of her tears, Laurette looks at him. "We'll come back!"

He jests, tenderly. Yes, Laurette; when one is of the crab, one does not break oneself in two forever. They have found one another once, although it was not easy. They will find one another again, somewhere...in time...

Somewhere? In Time? Vague formulas, but still too precise...

Perhaps, rather, outside of space and time? Who knows? Questions out of place... They will find one another. Yes, Laurette's anguished heart wants that, and cries out for it.

She caresses the children's hair and explains to them: "We're going to go, but we'll come back."

They look at her with indecisive smiles. Certainly, they have an intuition that the white gods are going to disappear. That is in conformity with all the traditions. But it is also in the order of things that those who are of the same blood do not part. How can these things be reconciled?

There is a difficulty in this that confounds their intelligence. Undoubtedly, the magic of the white gods will be able to cut through it.

Curious, Rara asks: "Will you come back tomorrow?"

Laurette shakes her head. Perhaps not tomorrow, or the next day, but after that.

After that?

It is vertiginous to envisage such distant perspectives. But since the divine sister accepts it, it must be for the best. However, in order to be entirely tranquil, it is necessary that the two gods be solemnly bound.

Rara is cunning. He knows the trick. He places his diaphanous palm on his breast and says, his voice coaxing: "Say like this: 'I promise Kroum. We will come back.'"

Docile, Laurette repeats after him: "I promise Kroum; we will come back."

Then Raramémé are quite content, and clap their hands. Getting up on tiptoe, they brush the white cheek with their dark red lips, with the pleasurable gesture that they did not know before, which the gods have taught them.

Laurette embraces them, hugging them fervently to her heart.

On Mémé's temple Rara points to the spot where the young woman's lips have just been placed. "Me, for you. Here. Tomorrow."

And Mémé, touching Rara's forehead, confirms: "Me. Tomorrow. There, for you."

Then they fall silent again. Since the divine sister— so pale, oh so pale!"—has spoken thus, all is well. Even so, their little hearts are beating irregularly. They huddle closer to the young woman, and, to reassure themselves, affirm politely: "You will come back? You have promised Kroum."

She returns their caresses and repeats, in a low voice: "I have promised Kroum. You can call him one last time."

The children intone:

Tick, tock,
Shock, crock...

One more time, the capricious song. One more time, from all the mysterious pools, all the dark holes in the coral, all the caverns in which they reside, the blue crabs stretch out their feet. The phalanx with the metallic back emerges, and advances noisily toward the young people at its oblique trot.

Rara digs his fingernails into Laurette's wrist.

"Say it to them too..."

Above the swarming mass, the young woman solemnly extends her excessively pale hand. "I have promised Kroum. We will come back."

One after another, pincers are raised and close with a click like castanets, reopen and close again.

Kroum has recorded the promise. At the supreme cry of "Kroum is alive!" the limping crabs move off again, clicking and clocking, going back to the waves and sinking thereinto.

Behind them, the gilded beach reappears, empty. Beyond the cape, the sun is sinking. The mountain is fuming redly. The bats are whistling and zigzagging.

A lugubrious clamor rises into the air: the call of the siren bellowing aboard the warship.

Cap in hand, the quartermaster Lancosme approaches.

"It's the ship, Captain..."

The Captain steadies his voice. "Let's go, Laurette. Be brave."

She makes no reply. She gets up, presses the two children to her bosom again, bursts into sobs, and allows herself to be drawn away.

Raraméme trot alongside without speaking. In the same way, one heart-rending day of their childhood, a lost dog trotted alongside them, accompanying them as far as the door of the old house, where it was necessary to abandon it to its destiny, to its solitude. It was only a dog...

Laurette clenches her teeth, leans on an extended arm, collapses on a bench, hides her face in her hands...

Her shoulders quiver. An order. The dinghy oscillates, glides away under the vigorous pressure of the oars.

In the stern, biting her handkerchief, the young woman raises her head and watches the two little bronze statues diminish, never ceasing to wave their little hands toward her, whose gilt fades away.

They quickly disappear, alas, melting into the thickening shadow. A shrill cry is sill audible, like the call of a seagull.

Lancosme mutters: "Poor kids!"

There is nothing more.

When the boat has sunk into the grayness for them, Raramémé have resumed crouching on the strand. They are very close together, but not close enough. The little warm thing that is beneath Mémé's left breast is palpitating, quivering.

Rara leans his cheek upon the spot, listens, and murmurs: "Oh, how your heart is hurting me!"

In a mechanical voice, Mémé stammers: "They will come back. They said so to Kroum."

He repeats: "She said so to Kroum. They will come back."

A heavy tread approaching does not make them turn around.

In recent days, Kouang has kept apart from the brown children and their friends. Has he suffered because of that intimacy, from which he feels partly-excluded? Is it a strange discretion that, for several days, has kept him in the woods and, just now, caused him to contemplate the departure at a distance, hidden on the edge of the coconut-palms?

Now that the children are alone again, and are in pain, he comes to them. Beneath his hairy torso palpitates that which is best in human consciousness. Many nights have passed since the children have abandoned he seaweed grotto for the threshold of the white gods. Today, perhaps they need to be protected again.

The monster places his enormous paw on the boy's shoulder, trying to draw him to him—but with a simultaneous start, the children push him back and turn away. "Go away!"

All night long they remain crouching, facing the sea over which the white gods are. That way, there are fewer barriers between them. Who knows where, by chance, something might yet emerge from the darkness? Over the water, a little star has lit up that the children do not know. It is shining where the whale-mountain is floating. They gaze at it avidly for a long time—a long time—until their eyelids close.

In the pale dawn they wake up, shivering. They do not speak. They watch. Slowly, the morning mist thins out, breaks up, dissipates, disappears...

The sea is empty. Far, far away, on the horizon, barely perceptible, there is a wisp of smoke—the last breath of the gods who are going away.

Where are they?

An unfathomable enigma. Are they wandering the seas, unattainably, in the mountain-pirogue? Or have they been absorbed already into the obscure diffuse entity from which Rahuo kneaded the world?

An unfathomable enigma against which there is only one recourse.

Religiously, Mémé weighs in her memory the magic words that fell from their lips: "They will come back."

And Rara repeats after her, looking out at the empty horizon: "They will come back."

And then, putting their little arms around one another, in order to warm themselves up and console one another, they sob, so closely united that there is now only one dolorous and tremulous creature of bronze.

VI. THE BLACK FLOWER

Through the vast swell of the Pacific, the violent blues of the Indian Ocean and the torrid Red Sea, the *Citoyen* pursues her course. She has only made two or three pauses at ports of call. As soon as she has taken aboard supplies of coal and water, she has resumed her rapid journey.

One might think that the European gulf were drawing her like an imperious magnet, already taking possession of all minds and all hearts. At every hour, the wireless transmits the latest news of the cataclysm. We have taken more prisoners on the Somme, but the offensive has not led to the anticipated breakthrough. Nothing much can be expected of the Russians. Sarrail is remaining in position in Salonika. Torpedo attacks are increasing. President Wilson, in his latest message, is addressing Germany in threatening terms. The Boche radio stations are announcing Islamic Holy War and an uprising in Egypt. At Suez, it is confirmed that there is agitation in Libya and that bands of Turks have appeared in the Sinai.[22] While the cruiser makes her way through the trench between the two deserts, her passengers contemplate the improvised trenches, the corrugated iron villag-

---

[22] These data allow the internal chronology of the story to be established with some precision. Maurice Sarrail's position as commander of the Allied forces in the so-called Macedonian theater was the subject of much controversy throughout 1916—he was eventually dismissed in December 1917—and the Arab Revolt against the Ottoman Empire began in June 1916.

es, the wooden barracks where the khaki-clad Australians, Indians of every shade and black camel-riders re encamped and enormous quantities of materiel are piled up. Seaplanes are circling incessantly in the sky.

The last halt is at Port Said, to fill the bunkers.

Ever since Oaleya, ceasing to be a tiny gray dot, has sunk into the immense ocean, Hugues de Pionne has lavished all the refinements of desperate tenderness on Laurette de Vesnage. Every day, that tenderness strives to be more enveloping, more fraternal; every day, it battles more vainly against the opaque cloud that has swallowed the young woman.

On deck, between the gun-turrets, a terrace has been improvised, with a chaise-longue covered by a canvas tent. She spends long hours there, cradled in an impenetrable dream. She only replies with a nod of the head, an inexpressive smile or a few mechanical syllables to the discreet greetings and words of banal amiability that Commandant de Kerfaouët, his officers, Dr. Boujade, the député and Monsieur Pittagol attempt to address to her in passing. One might think that on quitting the embalmed island, she has left behind the strength that she had found there, which had sustained her for a few weeks. As the distance that separates her from it increases, the young woman's complexion becomes more waxen, her cheeks pinker and more prominent, her coughing more frequent. And while the sources of life are drying up in her body, it seems that her mind is being absorbed, becoming indifferent to everything that surrounds her. She is not in pain, tries meekly to absorb a little nourishment, and smiles, but remains almost mute all day long, her eyes lost. From time to time her lips stir, sketching a remark, an embryonic response to obscure appeals.

Dr. Boujade has not concealed the seriousness of her condition from Hugues. In any case, the officer is under no illusion. He is glad that, in the mists in which she is wrapped, Laurette seems to have lost consciousness. Nevertheless, he would give, not his life—which does not belong to him—but everything else to cause a few supreme rays of joy to pass over her sweet face.

It is in vain, however, that, glossing over news of the universal nightmare and the anguish of the imminent separation, he tries to tell her how glad he will be to go, personally, when they disembark, to install the young woman in the old family home, in the midst of their shared memories. She lets him speak, approves distractedly, but seems unable to follow a thought that is escaping her...

Is it impossible, then, to illuminate her decline with a hope, some genteel trinket?

Facing the immobile scintillating lights of the port, Hugues leans over the livid hand and murmurs: "Laurette, I want to ask you something. As soon as I can get leave, will you marry me?"

At first she looks at him apathetically. Then a hint of astonishment lights up her gaze, and she replies, in a tone of amicable reprimand: "But Hugues, what would be the point?"

Since she welcomes the benevolent fiction anyway, it is necessary to maintain it.

"If only, Laurette, to ensure that conventions are respected when we both return to the fortunate isle to see whether Raramémé have not forgotten us."

Raramémé... Forgotten... The young woman's lips repeat the syllables. She closes her eyes, but opens them again with a glimmer of impish gaiety and puerile impatience: "What folly! It will be necessary to hurry, Hugues, to rush. We promised them, you know..."

And suddenly she is reanimated. She sits up. Her eyes shine.

"Hugues, it will be necessary not to take too much luggage. We'll take the Uncle's portrait, the illustrations of the crabs...and boxes of candy and chocolate...do you think that Kouang will like them? And Pippi-Kuink?"

Feverishly, the words press upon her lips. Anxiously, Hugues gazes at the delirious dying woman. He begs her: "Calm down, Laurette..."

She obeys, remains motionless, shivers, and seems to be cocking an ear. All her features contract, taking on an expression of suffering.

"Oh, Hugues, listen—how the little dears are calling us!"

She seizes his hand with unexpected force, and tries to get up.

"Are you coming?"

The *Citoyen* is ready to sail. In two or three days, she will reach Toulon—barring accidents, for navigation is scabrous. Only yesterday, two ships were torpedoed within sight of Alexandria. Several submarines have been sighted. There is every chance that the cruiser, traveling at full steam, will avoid their attack; nevertheless the danger exists, increased by the light of the moon, which will be full tomorrow.

All day long, softly, Laurette has been muttering. From her bloodless lips escape at intervals, not words, but bizarrely modulated syllables. With a constriction in his heart, Hugues has recognized them. They are the songs that Laurette has learned from the two wild children. There is the song of the octopus, the song of the ornithorhynchus...

Now, rising with the temperature of the fever, there is the cadenced refrain of Kroum, the crab fetish:

Tick, tock
Shock, crock...

Should he bless or curse the obsession of the magical island?

Toward evening, the agitation has declined. Laurette has opened brighter eyes, but complains that she is suffocating in her cabin.

With a thousand precautions, Dr. Boujade allows her to be carried on to the deck.

The night is indescribably splendid. All lights extinct, the *Citoyen* is traveling at top speed. The stars are scintillating violently. The silhouettes of sailors come and go, outlined pitch black against the silvery sheet projected by the moonlight.

Hugues is sitting silently on the afterdeck, next to the young woman's chaise-longue. There is an immense peace.

Between the romantic grace of the décor and the murder that is perhaps prowling close by, under the water, and between the beauty of the young woman haloed by the rays of the star and the agony that is breaking the man's heart, the contrast is too sharp. Involuntarily, the officer emits a groan.

He feels a light hand touch his own. "What's the matter, Hugues?"

He bites his lip and stammers, stupidly; "I wish we'd arrived, Laurette..."

"But why?" she protests.

He shakes his head. Why, indeed?

"All is well, Hugues," she continues. "Very well. It's necessary to accept. The children are waiting for us. We're going back. Since it's promised..."

And placidly, harmoniously, she becomes delirious...

Flick, flock...

Suddenly, a tremendous shock. The ship trembles, grates, rears up, falls back, oscillates with an enormous plaint. A muffled detonation. Then another. A long and strident ripping, like that of a gigantic piece of silk. Flames spring forth at the bow, immediately followed by a column of black smoke...

The pirate!

Hugues puts his head in his hands, races toward a cork object hanging from the planking.

"Quickly, Laurette, your lifebelt!"

In the midst of the crackling and the tumult of waters and voices, she reopens her eyes, and murmurs feebly: "What's the point?"

He seizes the light form in his arms, takes a step, and cries: "Help!"

But the detonations in the vessel's bow are succeeding one another, increasingly deafening. She is moaning in her entirety, shivering like a great beast, mortally wounded. There is no longer a deck underfoot. A great undulation precipitates the officer and his burden against the side-rail; he clings on to it.

In a host of clamors, Monsieur Le Guédec's warning can be distinguished: "We're sinking..." And now a supreme chorus rises up into the sky, in which the thunderous voice of Monsieur Bedeau-Conflans, which is, at that moment, not trembling, dominates all the rest: "*Vive la France!*"

Hugues hugs the young woman to him, impotently, seeking in vain for an impossible rescue.

But cheerful laughter melts into his ear. "Oh Hugues! How good it all is! Look—they're coming to meet us..."

Clinging to the officer, her face radiant with joy, the young woman watches the rising waves. Her finger points, over the silvery mass, at floating forms that become more precise...

Gripped by the suction of the sinking ship, innumerable phosphorescent crabs are surging forth, swirling, drawing nearer.

Triumphantly, Laurette stretches out her arms and utters a cry:

"Kroum is alive! Here we are..."

Then the sea swells up, becomes torrential, and bursts the petty carcass, whose fragments come apart. There is another detonation. The *Citoyen* struggles, projects her poop toward the sky, and then everything shatters, collides, scatters...and the wisps of straw laden with ants are definitely swallowed up, by the light the moonlit night, spangled with stars, into the midst of the peaceful sepulcher of the waves.

Now, above the scintillating waters, newly-liberated spirits are floating.

In Oaleya the Fortunate, the innocent Oyas have resumed the regular course of their existence. Already, the latest events that have troubled it are fading in their memory. Confused images float therein, in which what happened recently is mingled with distant legends, that which might have been, and all the rest...

In the memory of the tribe, the visit of the German submarine and that of the gods of the kiss retain an aspect scarcely more real than the action of Rahuo and the other tales of Polynesian mythology. The white gods have returned to the unknown and the inconceivable—as they should. The men retain a vague and fearful respect for them. The women have lost the taste for their caresses. All day long, the peaceful Oyas idle insouciantly in their forests, sheltering their games, their dreams and their fragile amours therein. In the evenings, they assemble amid dances and songs around a central fire, where they never tire of hearing Manga-Yaponi recite, indefinitely, the words that contain wisdom, history and knowledge.

Only Raramémé, apart from their people, pursue an obstinate search.

They have resumed their places in the cave of bats, with Kouang, every evening, but a single concern absorbs them.

Every day, at dawn, when their leaden eyes have hardly opened, they go out, run to the beach, and their sharp eyes scan the horizon, in search of the whale-mountain, until the last morning mists have dissolved.

Confronted by the empty ocean, the children are not discouraged. Perhaps it is by another route that it will please the gods to come back to them. At full tilt, Raramémé run to the site of the encampment, the last traces of whose debris are completing their disintegration. Nothing any longer remains of the visitors—not even their odor, effaced by the recent rains.

Then the children go in quest of traces on all the trails that they followed: on the bluff where the three-colored sign stands, in all the great thickets that fill the forest around the village, in the two coconut groves, all along the stream, in the caves where the bones of the giant birds lie, among the giant ferns, and on the banks of Taroa of the dormant waters.

In spite of their terror they have braved the burning breath of Hakarou, the volcano. On the southern headland, they have scrutinized the impassive visages of the sleeping stone gods, fruitlessly.

In spite of their repugnance, and in spite of the anguish that it caused them, small as they are—and frailer now, weakened by the departure of their big siblings—drawing away from their people, they have traversed the entire island. What if it were out there, near the ancestor's totem, that they must go to find them again?

The coral cross stands up, solitary. The children have knelt down before it, as the white gods did; as they did, they raise their brown hands to their tattooed foreheads and then to the blue designs on their breasts. Afterwards they have waited for a long time—a long time—until nightfall. In vain.

Anxiously—oh, how anxiously!—with their eyes, they voices, their ears, their noses and their gestures, Raramémé interrogate the grass, the trees, the animals, the stones, the ground. There is nothing so humble that the divine does not subsist within it. But the rocks have remained mute, and also the dust, and the grass, and the foliage, and the waters, and the winds. Pippi-kuink, whom Lauritea tamed, stuffs herself blissfully on slugs and worms that she no longer offers to him. Hop-klok the kangaroo parades his soft and inexpressive gaze over the children. Hra-koa the cockatoo loses himself in stupid, empty screeches.

Raramémé have summoned the people of Kroum. "Do you know anything about our white gods?"

The crabs have come running to the appeal, jostling, sticking out their round eyes, but in response to the questions asked of them, they only prance ridiculously, waving their pincers indecisively.

Irritated, the children chase them away with insults. Kroum returns, ashamed, to hide in his lairs.

At dusk, once again, the children hasten to the ruined camp—for, after all, who knows whether, during the day, having descended from the sky or sprung from the ground. Hougalauritea might not be there, waiting for them?

There is no sign of them. Then, very weary, silently, hand in hand, Raramémé return to Kouang's grotto.

The melancholy monster watches for them on the threshold, tries to cheer them up with amicable grunts. They do not respond to his advances, and fall asleep exhausted.

And as soon as sleep has closed their eyes, they are off of the quest again. Through the somber immensity, full of traps and perils, their spirits take flight and soar...

And sometimes, their constancy is rewarded. Yes, it sometimes happens that a frisson alerts them, that their nostrils quiver, that beloved hands reach through the darkness, extending toward them, that lips are placed on their moist foreheads. Sometimes, when they wake up, delightful words are still singing in their ears, with a inexpressible emphasis.

They continue quivering. Isolating themselves in the profound thickets all day long, they repeat them, again and again, listening in their hearts to the echoes that are dying away. Impatiently, feverishly, they wait for nightfall in order to resume their pursuit.

Who can tell whether, by virtue of patience and tenacity, they might not succeeded in getting a solid grip on those who have gone away, and bringing them back, in order to awaken in their bosom, in a suave dawn...

The days go by.

Every morning, Raramémé affirm: "They will come back."

To pensive Kouang, to Pippi-Kuink, to Kroum, and to all the others, they explain, at each encounter: "They will come back, you know." Thus their own certainty is confirmed. And the appeal of all, added to theirs, will exert a more powerful attraction on the cherished white gods.

Now, scarcely asleep, without hesitation, they depart. Such is the power of the sign of Kroum that neither darkness, nor the oceans, nor the fury of the winds, nor the jealousy of demons can separate those it unites. All the way to the edge of the great soft Entity, Raramémé rejoin Hougalauritea, hold them in their arms, stroke them, begging them: "Come back."

Oh, certainly—they have sworn by Kroum—the cherished gods want nothing more than to follow them, but even the gods are not masters of their actions. Other powers agitate around them, which hold them back. There are sticky things to clear away, bonds to beak, traps to escape, abysses to cross. One night is too short to triumph over so many spells, so many obstacles.

In the morning, Raramémé wake up exhausted, and the following night, it is all to do again...

It is necessary to remain nested, nested indefinitely beside the dear gods, patiently convincing them, taking them by the hand, on the lookout for the moment to escape the gulf together, to return together to the fresh light of Oaleya, the fortunate isle where Kroum is waiting.

One night—the one preceding the full moon—Raramémé have plunged much further, much further than usual into the magical slumber.

But this time, it is in vain.

In vain they struggle, strive and exhaust themselves, through fantastic deserts, sinking into gulfs, losing their breath in the empyrean. Around them, demons whirl, gripping them, paralyzing them. Cold breaths freeze them. Burning effluvia stifle them. They flinch, stumble. An entire hostile barrier looms up before them. Beyond it, Lauritea remains invisible; Houga too...

Should they give up, battle-weary?

Alas! From far away—oh! from what inexpressible beyond!—through the desolation of the empty sky, a double plaint rises toward them, which suddenly bursts forth with the din of a beaten gong.

Bewildered, covering in sweat, Raramémé awake.

In their breasts, their little twin hearts are beating atrociously.

Rara places his ear on Mémé's left breast, where the warm little beast is, and murmurs: "They're calling."

Palpitant, Mémé confirms: "Oh, how they're calling!"

Perplexed, Rara observes, querulously: "The route is difficult."

There is a silence. Then, with a single voice, both affirm: "We must help them."

In the darkness, the children get up, and slide noiselessly along the sleeping Kouang...

A livid patch indicates the exit from the cavern. Now they are standing up in the open air, in the moonlight. Their palms salute all the gods, imploring the forbearance of all the prowling spirits. And then, hand in hand, they bound through the brushwood, amid the immense silky swarm of nocturnal life.

From their lips, the song emerges that is only sung once:

> Rahuo has said: "You must be born,
> Oyas, love, drink, eat, greet the dawn...
> And when you have had enough of life.
> Taroa provides an end to strife...

One silver moon irradiates the sky. Another smiles on the calm waters of the sacred pool. Raramémé slip through the great thickets, where frightened birds wake up with a start. Nimbly, the little hands make a collection of flowers that are black. Very proud, Mémé brandishes her bouquet: "It's large." But Rara puffs himself up: "Mine's even larger."

Then, hand in hand, they go back.

> To love, to drink, to eat is prime
> Oyas delight therein for a time.
> Better still is the profound repose
> That the flower of Taroa bestows.

At the entrance to his hut, Manga-Yaponi is savoring the freshness of the dawn and indulging himself in polishing and turning over his wise thoughts.

Two puerile silhouettes loom up before him, prostrate themselves, and get up again. And four hands reached out to him, charged with sheaves the color of night.

"Very Great Father, we request the Black Flower."

The old man studies the children gravely. The Black Flower is the prerogative of all the Oyas, but it is usually only old people desirous of abbreviating their deterioration, the sick, the melancholy, or adventurous hunters, who dream of attempting the great voyage. It is almost unprecedented for children to claim it. Deprived of those of the crab, the tribe will be impoverished. Have they measured the solemnity of their action?

Gently, the old man says: "Children, there are delicious fruits in the woods, flowers that embalm, limpid waters, soft mosses, songbirds and butterflies like flying gemstones. Whomsoever drinks the Black Flower loses the joy of all that. Is it really the Black Flower that you are requesting?"

It really is. Raramémé bow down for a second time. And as the old man is the best, the wisest, they explain to him.

This is how it is: the very gentle white gods marked with the crab cannot remain distant from those of their sign. They are calling to them. Every night, across the immensity, the little spirits of Rararnémé go to join them. In the morning, with much difficulty, it is necessary to part from them. It is very tiring. When the children wake up, their limbs are exhausted. They no longer have any appetite. The god Rongo-mai shakes their breasts. They are sad.

Last night, the call of the white gods was more imperious. It is necessary to obey. When they have drunk the Black Flower, Rararnémé will be free, not only to join them, but to remain with them for the necessary time. Who can tell—perhaps they will all come back together to the fortunate isle?

Maga-Yaponi turns these words over and over in the crucible of his spirit. He reveres the intuition that comes from the crab. The tradition of which he is the custodian suggests the appropriate commentary. It is in the order of things that the white gods should demand another tribute in order to spare Oaleya. The sacrifice of Mao, on its own, could not appease them. It will be completed by that of the two children. The blood of the crab will thus fall silent in Oaleya, which is a great loss, but the will of the All-Powerful cannot be contradicted.

In consequence Manga-Yaponi nods his white-haired head in a sign of assent, and pronounces: "This evening, before sunset, I will give you the Black Flower. Make your adieux."

Raramémé leap with joy, clapping their hands, thanking the patriarch exuberantly, and, in conformity with custom—for it is necessary to be very polite—they make the round of their visits.

They go from hut to hut, saluting the members of all the totems and receiving their messages for those of their blood who are already wandering in the poorly-known regions, and whom they might perhaps encounter. Because of the ancestral rivalry, only the people of the octopus turn their heads away as they approach. All the other clans welcome them amicably, formulating their desires and blessings. Let Raramémé invite the demons to cease gnawing Taoré's leg and selling Kittea's belly, which has become very hard. Several women entrust them with words for the white gods who have deigned to approach them. Children contemplate Raramémé enviously, who have been summoned by the spirits so young. Adults give them useful advice. The old, who are sometimes so strangely attached to life, rejoice that perhaps the sacrifice of the crab will satiate the gods and deter them from demanding other victims for a time.

Having saluted the humans, Raramémé go to take their leave of animals and things. They salute the earth with which their bones will be molded. They salute the trees whose fruits are so tasty, the variegated flowers, the mosses that were soft against their bodies, the roots that were good to their stomachs, the waters that slaked their thirst deliciously, and the breezes that embalmed their lungs. Adieu to the squirrel, the kangaroo, the modest kiwi. Adieu, laughing, to the loquacious parrots and the ever-agile macaques.

One last time, Raramémé roll Pippi-kuink playfully in the mud, who seethes and hisses. Come on, Tiparu the armadillo, just for today, poke your nose through the window of your carapace and don't sulk. Tomorrow, no one will tickle you anymore.

There is one more great adieu to Kouang. Perhaps, in recent times, the children's minds have often strayed far from him. It is not their fault. They apologize, explain, and politely ask his forgiveness. In order that he will not be sad, they stay with him throughout their last day. They idle, eat and take their siesta together.

Kouang does not grasp the detail of that speech. But this is certain: their hands are caressing him and their hearts are pressing next to his. A tender emotion uplifts he giant's heart. Has there been such a pleasant day since Koua was snatched away from him? He joins in their games with a naïve gaiety. They run, they hide, they chase one another, they climb, they jostle, they argue over fruits.

Mémé coughs, exhausted and out of breath. In the end, beneath a mulberry bush, the children, overcome by fatigue, fall down and go to sleep beside the monster. He gazes at them blissfully, glad to have them to himself again. After an hour, leaving them asleep, he goes away in order to hunt, as is his custom, for the roots that are solely capable of maintaining his vigor.

When Raramémé wake up, the sun is already low in the sky. Mémé stretches, yawns, peers idly at the parrots quarreling in the foliage. But Rara's voice tickles her ear. "Mémé is asleep. I'm going on my own to drink the Black Flower. She sits up suddenly, frowns and gets annoyed. He laughs at the success of his teasing. She bites his shoulder, growling, in order to pretend to be very angry, and takes his hand—and they both run to the old man's hut.

He is squatting on the threshold. In a great calabash he is completing the preparation of the magic beverage. All day, the chosen herbs have been simmering in palm juice over a small fire, while has periodically incorporated secret virtues in them by means of irresistible words. He crushes them carefully with a bone pestle. Three times the liquid boils and rises up. Heady vapors are emitted in violet spirals. The elixir is ready. The old man hands it to Raramémé. Each of them is to drink half.

And he blesses them. "Return among the gods. Let them not be irritated with the Oyas, since, in order to please them, we are sending them the best of our blood."

The children salute the sage very politely and go away. The walk very slowly, biting their tongues in concentration, in order not to spill a drop of the precious potion.

Here is the beach of golden sand. The tide is already very low. The black heads of the coral are dotting the waves. Raramémé put the calabash down in the sand, carefully, and one last time, clapping their hands, launch the appeal:

Click, clock,
Knock, shock,

Are we asleep
In the deep?

At the call of their race, the blue crabs come out of
their lairs, rejoicing, trotting sideways. In a few minutes,
the circle has formed. The large protruding eyes are directed at the children. And Rara harangues his people.
The hour has come. The white gods of the crab are calling. Water, earth and sky cannot separate those whom
the sign unites. Soon, the spirit of Raramémé will take
flight toward their brethren, in the Unknown. Let Kroum
take responsibility for what will remain lying on the
golden sand. Kroum is alive!

"Kroum is alive!" Once again, with a single gesture,
the blue crabs stand up on their feet, waving their pincers, making them click, and then at a precipitate trot,
return to their retreat while the rhythmic chant accompanies their flight.

Click, clock,
Block, mock,
Shall we go
Back down below?
To take our pride
Away to hide;
Blood will survive!
Kroum is alive!

The setting sun extends its final flames. Raramémé
remain alone before its splendor. There is a divine serenity in the air. Are not tender, amicable, fraternal spirits
already fluttering around those who are about to depart?

Teasingly, however, the children argue. Each of
them, greedily, wants to drink the precious beverage

first. Mémé, annoyed, sulks and pulls a nasty face. Naturally, she will give in if Rara demands it, since he is the stronger—but no. Rara will not abuse his preeminence. Has he not always reserved for Mémé the tastiest fruits, the most succulent roots? Mémé will drink first, but only the half that is hers. Then, very politely, her spirit will wait for Rara's, in order that they might go away together.

Agreed. Once again, they exchange between them the exceedingly pleasant gesture that the white gods have taught them. Then, obligingly, Rara raises the cup of repose to Mémé's lips. She applies her lips to it sagely, drinks in long sips. There it is, half empty.

Rara takes back the calabash and, before drinking in his turn, looks at his little sister. The little girl's eyes are becoming vague, misting, rolling slightly. There is a smile on her lips. Then, suddenly, she becomes pale. Oh, how pale she is becoming! What is there in the depths of her pupils that is changing and sinking? Mémé vacillates, lies down lazily and murmurs: "I'm coming."

She will not go without him, the naughty girl!

With a greedy gesture, Rara raises the cup to his own lips.

He does not have time to drink. His arm has fallen back, devoid of strength. He collapses in a heap, without a whimper, and the sand drinks the spilled liquid. For the precious little beast that Mémé had given him has ceased to palpitate in her left breast. At a stroke, without having touched a drop of the poison, Rara has already died, of Mémé's death.

In small surges, and petty waves, implacable and eternal, the tide comes in. The waves sing, prance, race, chanting the eternal hymn that they repeat relentlessly, century after century. They sing, climb, rise. Far away, insouciantly, they have swallowed Hugues and Laurette, impalpable grains that are dissolving. Here, gently, implacably, they rise, leaping over one another, brushing the summits of rocks, covering them—and their foam is already licking two little brown heads on the sand.

On the edge of the coconut grove the silhouette of Kouang appears. He catches sight of the double patch at the water's edge. They are still asleep, the lazy children. He approaches them in order to tickle them. His eyes flatten. His hair bristles. A frisson runs down his back and he leans over with a hoarse exclamation. The two little bodies, which were so warm, are cold...

The sea sings, sells, pushing its wavelets ever higher, ever further. Already, it is feeling the coppery bodies, crawling along their limbs. Are they not hideous octopodes projecting their tentacles? But no, a vast splashing surges from the surface of the waves. Somber disks emerge, bristling with backs, feet and pincers. In their entirety, the people of Kroum have come running. They form a circle around Raramémé. The most robust dig into the sand, insinuate themselves beneath them, brace themselves, and lift them up.

The sea sings. Its wavelets race, redoubling, and—giddy up!—assist the crabs in depositing the brown burden on their backs.

And now, in a long and powerful surge, the whole slides, sinks and disappears.

Above the waves, in the descending darkness, Kouang has taken refuge on a coral promontory.

If Dr. Klagenmeyer could see him, he would note with appropriate interest one curious detail: oozing from the brute's eyes are drops of the liquid that the special glands of a few mammals distill, and which humans call tears.

212

And from the formidable breast, a dull plaint escapes indefinitely: a vague and desperate malediction, directed at the Eternal...

And, insensibly, the Eternal replies:

"Silence...
"There is me.
"Me, that's all.
"What do I hear?
"Mosquitoes?
"Empires crumbling?
"A deluge?
"Or, in the ether, the grating of whirling stars?
"Or did I belch?
"There is me. I am because I am. That's it. Everything is. Everything has been, everything will be. There is, perpetually, becoming. Me. That's all. That's the way it is. Damn the rest. Anyway, there is no rest. Me, that's all. I roll. I swallow. I digest. Here I am again. It's me. It's you. Us. Everything.

"Nothingness? Atua? One of my pseudonyms. A hollow bubble. There's me. Always and everywhere.

The creator? Rahuo? One of my false noses. A joke. Yes, it amuses me to spit out planets here and there, and civilizations. One amuses oneself as one can.

You who suffer, moan, think, pray—shut up. You bore me. Stop whining.

What? Your name is Plato? Pascal? Goethe? France? Humanity? Don't know you. Have I the time to count the lice upon my lice and give them names? I scratch myself.

"There's me. My perpetual snore, from the breath of which, without my noticing, worlds are born, rotate and collapse, with their knick-knacks and their mites. The universe that you conceive is one of my frissons. I've just sneezed out a few dozen more.

"You too, dear. Be proud. The least of your bowel movements is a genesis and an apocalypse. You shout your works, your virtues, your genius at me. Easy, now. Known. If you knew! In the gut of one of the bacilli that's already gnawing your marrow, there's a darling of a little solar system, every earth of which is pregnant with several Shakespeares. What if all of them made as much racket as you!

"In truth, you fidget even more than those diabolical corals that have built you a continent before you have time to turn round.

"Don't cling. Let yourself go. Yesterday, your mother, the Moneron, gave birth to you. Little imp! And here you are, already, finishing, dissolving the bones of your great-grand-nephews under frozen ground denuded of humans.

"Anyway, it happens. It's all the same to me. Worlds: born, live, die, engender in dying. Shivers. Smoke. Scoria. There's me, who breathes and rolls, incessantly, forever—forever, you hear?—there'll be me.

"There is no nothingness.

"There is no Creator.

"There is no individual.

"There is no repose.

"There is me, the eternal oven, God and slave-laborer, me and my sweat, each bitter drop of which contains a world of worlds and of suffering.

"But it's already wiped away.

"Whose turn is it now?"

SF & FANTASY

Henri Allorge. *The Great Cataclysm*
Guy d'Armen. *Doc Ardan: The City of Gold and Lepers*
G.-J. Arnaud. *The Ice Company*
Charles Asselineau. *The Double Life*
Cyprien Bérard. *The Vampire Lord Ruthwen*
Aloysius Bertrand. *Gaspard de la Nuit*
Richard Bessière. *The Gardens of the Apocalypse*
Albert Bleunard. *Ever Smaller*
Félix Bodin. *The Novel of the Future*
Louis Boussenard. *Monsieur Synthesis*
Alphonse Brown. *City of Glass; The Conquest of the Air*
Emile Calvet. *In a Thousand Years*
André Caroff. *The Terror of Madame Atomos; Miss Atomos; The Return of Madame Atomos; The Mistake of Madame Atomos; The Monsters of Madame Atomos; The Revenge of Madame Atomos; The Resurrection of Madame Atomos*
Félicien Champsaur. *The Human Arrow; Ouha, King of the Apes; Pharaoh's Wife*
Didier de Chousy. *Ignis*
Michel Corday. *The Eternal Flame*
Captain Danrit. *Undersea Odyssey*
C. I. Defontenay. *Star (Psi Cassiopeia)*
Charles Derennes. *The People of the Pole*
Georges Dodds (anthologist). *The Missing Link*
Harry Dickson. *The Heir of Dracula*
Jules Dornay. *Lord Ruthven Begins*
Alfred Driou. *The Adventures of a Parisian Aeronaut*
Sâr Dubnotal *vs. Jack the Ripper*
Alexandre Dumas. *The Return of Lord Ruthven*
Renée Dunan. *Baal*
J.-C. Dunyach. *The Night Orchid; The Thieves of Silence*
Henri Duvernois. *The Man Who Found Himself*
Achille Eyraud. *Voyage to Venus*
Henri Falk. *The Age of Lead*
Paul Féval. *Anne of the Isles; Knightshade; Revenants; Vampire City; The Vampire Countess; The Wandering Jew's Daughter*
Paul Féval, *fils. Felifax, the Tiger-Man*
Charles de Fieux. *Lamékis*

Arnould Galopin. *Doctor Omega*; *Doctor Omega and the Shadowmen* (anthology)
Judith Gautier. *Isoline and the Serpent-Flower*
Léon Gozlan. *The Vampire of the Val-de-Grâce*
G.L. Gick. *Harry Dickson and the Werewolf of Rutherford Grange*
Edmond Haraucourt. *Illusions of Immortality*
Nathalie Henneberg. *The Green Gods*
V. Hugo, P. Foucher & P. Meurice. *The Hunchback of Notre-Dame*
Romain d'Huissier. *Hexagon: Dark Matter*
Michel Jeury. *Chronolysis*
Gustave Kahn. *The Tale of Gold and Silence*
Gérard Klein. *The Mote in Time's Eye*
Fernand Kolney. *Love in 5000 Years*
Paul Lacroix. *Danse Macabre*
Louis-Guillaume de La Follie. *The Unpretentious Philosopher*
Jean de La Hire. *Enter the Nyctalope; The Nyctalope on Mars; The Nyctalope vs. Lucifer; The Nyctalope Steps In; Night of the Nyctalope*
Etienne-Léon de Lamothe-Langon. *The Virgin Vampire*
André Laurie. *Spiridon*
Gabriel de Lautrec. *The Vengeance of the Oval Portrait*
Alain le Drimeur. *The Future City*
Georges Le Faure & Henri de Graffigny. *The Extraordinary Adventures of a Russian Scientist Across the Solar System* (2 vols.)
Gustave Le Rouge. *The Vampires of Mars; The Dominion of the World* (w/Gustave Guitton) (4 vols.)
Jules Lermina. *Mysteryville; Panic in Paris; To-Ho and the Gold Destroyers; The Secret of Zippelius*
André Lichtenberger. *The Centaurs; The Children of the Crab*
Jean-Marc & Randy Lofficier. *Edgar Allan Poe on Mars; The Katrina Protocol; Pacifica; Robonocchio; Tales of the Shadowmen 1-9*
Xavier Mauméjean. *The League of Heroes*
Joseph Méry. *The Tower of Destiny*
Hippolyte Mettais. *The Year 5865*
Louise Michel. *The Human Microbes; The New World*
Tony Moilin. *Paris in the Year 2000*
José Moselli. *Illa's End*
John-Antoine Nau. *Enemy Force*
Marie Nizet. *Captain Vampire*
C. Nodier, A. Beraud & Toussaint-Merle. *Frankenstein*
Henri de Parville. *An Inhabitant of the Planet Mars*
Gaston de Pawlowski. *Journey to the Land of the 4th Dimension*

Georges Pellerin. *The World in 2000 Years*
Ernest Pérochon. *The Frenetic People*
Pierre Pelot. *The Child Who Walked on the Sky*
J. Polidori, C. Nodier, E. Scribe. *Lord Ruthven the Vampire*
P.-A. Ponson du Terrail. *The Vampire and the Devil's Son; The Immortal Woman*
Henri de Régnier. *A Surfeit of Mirrors*
Maurice Renard. *The Blue Peril; Doctor Lerne; The Doctored Man; A Man Among the Microbes; The Master of Light*
Jean Richepin. *The Wing; The Crazy Corner*
Albert Robida. *The Adventures of Saturnin Farandoul; The Clock of the Centuries; Chalet in the Sky; The Electric Life*
J.-H. Rosny Aîné. *Helgvor of the Blue River; The Givreuse Enigma; The Mysterious Force; The Navigators of Space; Vamireh; The World of the Variants; The Young Vampire*
Marcel Rouff. *Journey to the Inverted World*
Han Ryner. *The Superhumans*
Brian Stableford. *The New Faust at the Tragicomique;The Empire of the Necromancers (The Shadow of Frankenstein; Frankenstein and the Vampire Countess; Frankenstein in London); Sherlock Holmes & The Vampires of Eternity; The Stones of Camelot; The Wayward Muse.* (anthologist) *The Germans on Venus; News from the Moon; The Supreme Progress; The World Above the World; Nemoville; Investigations of the Future*
Jacques Spitz. *The Eye of Purgatory*
Kurt Steiner. *Ortog*
Eugène Thébault. *Radio-Terror*
C.-F. Tiphaigne de La Roche. *Amilec*
Théo Varlet. *The Golden Rock. The Xenobiotic Invasion; The Castaways of Eros; Timeslip Troopers* (w/André Blandin); *The Martian Epic* (w/Octave Joncquel)
Paul Vibert. *The Mysterious Fluid*
Villiers de l'Isle-Adam. *The Scaffold; The Vampire Soul*
Philippe Ward. *Artahe*
Philippe Ward & Sylvie Miller. *The Song of Montségur*

MYSTERIES & THRILLERS

M. Allain & P. Souvestre. *The Daughter of Fantômas*
A. Anicet-Bourgeois, Lucien Dabril. *Rocambole*

A. Bernède. *Belphegor*; *Judex* (w/Louis Feuillade); *The Return of Judex* (w/Louis Feuillade); *The Shadow of Judex*

A. Bisson & G. Livet. *Nick Carter vs. Fantômas*

V. Darlay & H. de Gorsse. *Arsène Lupin vs. Sherlock Holmes: The Stage Play*

Séamas Duffy. *Sherlock Holmes in Paris*

Paul Féval. *Gentlemen of the Night; John Devil; The Black Coats ('Salem Street; The Invisible Weapon; The Parisian Jungle; The Companions of the Treasure; Heart of Steel; The Cadet Gang; The Sword-Swallower)*

Emile Gaboriau. *Monsieur Lecoq*

Goron & Emile Gautier. *Spawn of the Penitentiary*

Rick Lai. *Shadows of the Opera: Retribution in Blood*

Steve Leadley. *Sherlock Holmes: The Circle of Blood*

Maurice Leblanc. *Arsène Lupin vs. Countess Cagliostro; Arsène Lupin vs. Sherlock Holmes (The Blonde Phantom; The Hollow Needle); The Many Faces of Arsène Lupin*

Gaston Leroux. *Chéri-Bibi; The Phantom of the Opera; Rouletabille & the Mystery of the Yellow Room; Rouletabille at Krupp's*

Richard Marsh. *The Complete Adventures of Judith Lee*

William Patrick Maynard. *The Terror of Fu Manchu; The Destiny of Fu Manchu*

Frank J. Morlock. *Sherlock Holmes: The Grand Horizontals; Sherlock Holmes vs Jack the Ripper*

Antonin Reschal. *The Adventures of Miss Boston*

P. de Wattyne & Y. Walter. *Sherlock Holmes vs. Fantômas*

David White. *Fantômas in America*

Pierre Yrondy. *The Adventures of Thérèse Arnaud*

SCREENPLAYS

Mike Baron. *The Iron Triangle*

Emma Bull & Will Shetterly. *Nightspeeder; War for the Oaks*

Gerry Conway & Roy Thomas. *Doc Dynamo*

Steve Englehart. *Majorca*

James Hudnall. *The Devastator*

Jean-Marc & Randy Lofficier. *Royal Flush*

J.-M. & R. Lofficier & Marc Agapit. *Despair*

J.-M. & R. Lofficier & Joël Houssin. *City*

Andrew Paquette. *Peripheral Vision*

Robert L. Robinson, Jr. *Judex*

R. Thomas, J. Hendler & L. Sprague de Camp. *Rivers of Time*

NON-FICTION

Stephen R. Bissette. *Blur 1-5. Green Mountain Cinema 1; Teen Angels*
Win Scott Eckert. *Crossovers* (2 vols.)
Jean-Marc & Randy Lofficier. *Shadowmen* (2 vols.)
Randy Lofficier. *Over Here*

ART BOOKS

Jean-Pierre Normand. *Science Fiction Illustrations*
Raven Okeefe. *Raven's L'il Critters; Rave's Faves*
Randy Lofficier & Raven Okeefe. *If Your Possum Go Daylight...*
Daniele Serra. *Illusions*

HEXAGON COMICS

Franco Frescura & Luciano Bernasconi. *Wampus*
Franco Frescura & Giorgio Trevisan. *CLASH*
L. Bernasconi, J.-M. Lofficier & Juan Roncagliolo Berger. *Phenix*
Claude Legrand, J.-M. Lofficier & L. Bernasconi. *Kabur*
Franco Oneta. *Zembla*
L. Buffolente, Lofficier & J.-J. Dzialowski. *Strangers: Homicron*
Danilo Grossi. *Strangers: Jaydee*
Claude Legrand & Luciano Bernasconi. *Strangers: Starlock*

www.ingramcontent.com/pod-product-compliance
Lightning Source LLC
Chambersburg PA
CBHW060358030726
47497CB00003B/765

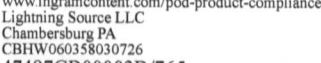